AND YET

JEFF ALESSANDRELLI

Printed in the United States of America

First Edition
1 2 3 4 5 6 7 8 9

Cover design by Sasha Ori

Library of Congress Cataloging-in-Publication Data

ISBN978-1-948587-23-5

PANK Magazine
PANK Books

To purchase multiple copies or book events, readings and author signings contact awesome@pankmagazine.com.

AND YET

JEFF ALESSANDRELLI

Also by Jeff Alessandrelli

Erik Satie Watusies His Way Into Sound

THIS LAST TIME WILL BE THE FIRST

The Man on High: Essays on Skateboarding, Hip-Hop, Poetry and The Notorious B.I.G. (U.K.)

Fur Not Light

Nothing of the Month Club (U.K.)

I dreamed of writing a book about sexual fear. It would involve a capable and attractive male protagonist who, nevertheless, experienced a form of near paralysis when it came to sex and the sexual act. Taking place over a period of 10+ years, that protagonist would find comfort and solace in art and literature, in his own exploratory ruminations, in the endless examination of his own endless self. After starts and roundabouts and stops, the ending of the book would—well, the ending would have to be arrived at in a way I knew not how, at least not in the early stage dreaming.

"Sexual pleasure is offered to man by life as an incomparable blessing. The moment of the sexual act is one of resolution and gushing forth—it presents the perfect image of happiness," states Georges Bataille in the first paragraph of his essay "Happiness, Eroticism and Literature." What happens, I thought, if that was reversed— pleasure as curse and resolution as trembled timidity?

Thus *And Yet*. The first draft of it was completed in Fall 2018, just a few months before Kate Julian's "Why Are Young People Having So Little Sex?" story appeared on the cover of the December 2018 issue of *The Atlantic*. ("Despite the easing of taboos and the rise of hookup apps, Americans are in the midst of a sex recession" read the deliberately provocative subtitle of Julian's piece.) Since the publication of Julian's article publications as disparate as *The Guardian, the Institute for Family Studies, Vox, Psychology Today* and *Cosmopolitan* have all weighed in on the "sex recession," debating, confirming, refuting, relentlessly pontificating. The consensus? It's murky, quite murky, and in terms of clarity the Covid-19 pandemic hasn't helped matters much either. What does seem to be true, however, is that which has always been true, namely that one's sexual sensibility and sexual notions are extraordinarily idiosyncratic and nuanced. No one or nothing can be generalized. (Which doesn't mean that it doesn't happen every day, all the time, 24-7.)

And Yet exists within the world that Kate Julian's article laid out, while nevertheless being completely apart from it. Although an emotional truth to the book exists, and all of the literary and artistic references and quotations/citations are completely true, *And Yet* is fictional in scope, with imagined people, places and ways of being. In a 2010 interview the writer/musician David Berman (RIP) and James Tate (RIP) exchanged the below back and forth:

DB: In a 1982 interview, you said, "The I, of course is never autobiographical." Twenty-eight years later, I ask you: isn't your poetry at least 5 percent autobiographical?

JT: I'd say 1 percent.

Like Tate, the "I" protagonist contained within *And Yet* is at least 1 percent autobiographical. The other 99 percent, though, consists of speculation and wholly unverifiable creative "fact." The I is an Everyman of sorts, albeit a peculiar one, for a peculiar time. As paraphrased from the first line of the poet John Gallaher's poem "The Way We Live Now," to tell as much of the truth as I could imagine was my edict while writing *And Yet*. As much of the truth as I could possibly imagine.

The final issue worth addressing is, of course, the most salient one. Simply—why in the world write a book like this? Filled with seemingly predetermined perversion and salacious oddity, why? It's because I was interested in the tension of desire, thwarted or unthwarted desire. Sexual desire, sure, but really any type of desire, particularly those that seem to fester rather than break free or snap taut. And no matter who you are (or aren't), what you do (or don't do), or what you believe (or don't believe), everyone feels such tensions, whether they choose to acknowledge them or not.

8/13/21

"I am not overwhelmed by the question of sex. I dominate it in the name of love."— André Breton.

***

"I am only interested in people engaged in a project of self-transformation."
—Susan Sontag.

***

"The instability of human knowledge is one of our few certainties. Almost everything we know we know incompletely at best."—Janet Malcolm.

For (most) everyone and (most) no one

*

I don't fear sex. Or love. Not exactly. Rather, I fear not truly understanding the title of Jane's Addiction's classic 1988 album *Nothing's Shocking*, where Perry Farrell's reedy, distinctive yelp on songs like "Jane Says" and "Mountain Song" euphoniously marries itself to Dave Navarro's nimble guitar lines, to Eric Avery's syncopated slap-bass and Stephen Perkins' steady percussion. Of not understanding *Nothing's Shocking* album cover, a (not) shocking sculpture of nude female conjoined twins, large breasts prevalent, on an oversized rocking chair with their heads engulfed in billowing flame. Laden with tributaries, I fear having—or choosing—to exist in the glibness of those previous sentences because of what I might lack.

*

On the occasions when someone has sent me a nude pic, I've studied and studied, then sent it right back to them. Their response has told me far more than their physical nakedness has.

*

In a world where one's erotic capital increasingly matters as much as one's economic capital, prudery is shocking, no matter if one is young (18+) or old. Sexual shyness, reticence, priggishness, puritanism, some unfleeting exclusiveness to one's own endless self. But where, in Western culture at least, sex is everywhere, ubiquitous— streaming, scrolling, swipeable— such unthinkable states and emotions are increasingly prevalent. Compared to the Baby Boomer generation and Generation X, Millennials become sexually active later in life and sleep with fewer people. Dating and marriage occurs later in their lives, as does childbirth. Sexual prolificity is less important than personal identity, comfort and security.

*

As a Millennial, what I want is my self, my freely-sustained fully-possible self, and the path to such knowledge dwindles the more I fuck you. And you. And you.

And you.

*

I'm selfish in other words, but only in relation to my estimation of what everyone else lacks.

*

Is it a privilege to write about what one fears most? To freely open oneself up to all attendant interior apprehensions and plug ahead anyway?

*

Rapper Young Thug on his sexual inclinations with fiancée Jerrika Karlae:

"'"We wasn't doing it on like no it's too early to have sex shit,'" he explains. "'I don't care for sex that much. I've never actually had sex with her. Never ever. Our first time doin' grown stuff, she did it. She pulled me to the room and was like 'come here.'"'

"'Karlae stated that initially she thought he was "weird" for not having sex, but went on to explain why that made her more attracted to Thugga."'

To be fair, Young Thug—born August 16, 1991—has six children by four different women and in 2018 announced a new name change, to SEX.

*

And yet.

*

> "She was a brain researcher and an authority on the scientific basis of love. He, too, was a neuroscientist, but with an expertise in loneliness. She was in her mid-30s, he in his late 50s.
>
> Both were wedded to careers in separate hemispheres—until they happened to be seated beside each other, serendipitously, at dinner on the last night of a neuroscience research symposium in Shanghai."

So begins the *New York Times* obituary for John Cacioppo, co-author of the seminal text *Loneliness: Human Nature and the Need for Social Connections*. The piece ends with a quote from the widowed Dr. Stephanie Cacioppo (née Ortigue): "I did not know what true love was until I met my husband. John taught me what true love really means. And now, thanks to my husband, I am on the verge of knowing what true eternal love is."

*

Is it a curse, such a privilege?

*

True eternal love. A type of love that I can only assume becomes eternal by din of a passion—physical, emotional, spiritual—that refuses all manners of temporal cynicism. Still, there's that verge to consider. What happens if Dr. Cacioppo never makes it around the bend, instead capitulating to mere earthly love, a love that, twenty-five years from now, her husband in the ground for twenty-five years, suddenly falters. What if she meets the second love of her life tomorrow and does not have the wherewithal to recognize it?

"The closer I come to you
In reality
The more does the key sing in the door of the unknown room
. . .
There is a silk ladder unrolled over the ivy
There is
Hopeless fusion of your presence and your absence
I have found the secret
Of loving you
Always for the first time"

From his poem "Always For the First Time," these are the Surrealist poet André Breton's thoughts regarding love in this life and the next. By wholly loving, Breton asserts, we lose what any definition of love might be; innocence piled upon innocence takes its place.

*

Eternally true.

*

Is the ultimate privilege of all being able to *choose* what one fears most?

*

A noted misogynist—"The problem of woman," he wrote in 1929, "is the most marvelous and disturbing problem in all the world"— André Breton was married three times. Although artistically talented in their own rights, each of his wives—Simone Collinet, Jacqueline Lamba and Elisa Bindhoff—was habitually referred to as "Breton's wife" or simply "her."

*

Prudence is the ability to govern and discipline oneself via the use of calibrated reason; to be prudent is to be marked by wisdom and judiciousness. Thus prudery, by extension, should be a laudable concept, some much-commended character trait entailing sagacity, tact and decorum. I thought I'd try and redefine the word in order to accommodate my own reservations about it! But then I realized.

*

Published in the *Personality and Social Psychology Bulletin* in 1997 by the psychologist Arthur Aron (among others) and regularly cited since, "The Experimental Generation of Interpersonal Closeness: A Procedure and Some Preliminary Findings" is a primer of scientific inquiry on comfortability and intimacy, one that, at its end, lists thirty-six "closeness-generating procedure" questions. Made famous by Mandy Len Catron's 2015 *Modern Love* essay "To Fall in Love With Anyone, Do This," Aron's inquiry includes questions such as *11. Take 4 minutes and tell your partner your life story in as much detail as possible, 10. If you could change anything about the way you were raised, what would it be?* and *32. What, if anything, is too serious to be joked about?*

As originally conceived, however, "The Experimental Generation of Interpersonal Closeness…" and its probing thirty-six questions were not designed to induce love but familiarity and closeness; "we had not created the 36 questions to help you fall in love" is how Elaine Aron, Arthur Aron's wife and a co-author of the paper, put it. No matter how close you are with someone, closeness is never love, and love is never truly about itself.

In this way those thirty-six questions resemble Andreas Capellanus's 31 Rules of Love as identified by the "King of Love" in Capellanus's 12th century volume *The Art of Courtly Love*. Although some of King of Love's rules are, of course, chivalric products of the author's particular time and era—*VII. When one lover dies, a widowhood of two years is required of the survivor* and *XXV. A true lover considers nothing good except what he thinks will please his beloved*—many of them are abstract and amorphous, of the ilk that can still be read today in supermarket magazines and tabloids: *XIV. The easy attainment of love makes it of little value; difficulty of attainment makes it prized. XIX. If love diminishes, it quickly fails and rarely revives. XVII. A new love puts flight to an old one.* Although such proclamations might seem cliché now, in Capellanus's era they were eye-opening, regardless of whether one believed wholeheartedly in the rules set down by the "King of Love" or found them suspicious, insistent on too much and too little at the same time.

Perhaps surprisingly, though, many of the 31 Rules involve qualities of apprehension and vexation, with jealousy being the most common through-word. *II. He who is not jealous cannot love* and *XXI. Real jealousy always increases the feeling of love* and *XXII. Jealousy, and therefore love, are increased when one suspects his beloved* and *XXVIII. A slight presumption causes a lover to suspect his beloved.* In the same way that Aron's thirty-six questions to help you fall in love were not designed for that purpose, wrongly conflating closeness and comfortability with passion and ardor, Capellanus's 31 Rules of Love leave the present-day reader with the idea that true love, eternal, is less a matter of endearment and affection and more one of uncertainty and indecision. To never truly know and to be, happily or unhappily, forced to live—love— in that unknowingness, life entire.

*

Then I realized that most redefinitions only serve to reinforce the bald articulation of the primary definition, that one most well-known.

*

And yet.

*

"When boys tell me I'm a prude, I say, 'You're absolutely right. I cultivate it,'" imparts Magdalen, one of the characters in Mary Gaitskill's famed story collection *Bad Behavior*. She says it with a zest simultaneously becoming and unbecoming of a young woman intent on her own destruction. She says it with the profligacy of a young woman who isn't sure who she is and aims to find out by fucking, lying through her teeth and fucking.

*

That type of cultivation, the only type.

*

Tentative, unsure, constantly navigating the contours of what one wants to do vs. what one thinks should be done, insistent on being honest and forthright while yet taking care to coat such candor in a veneer of proprietary deference inlaid by rigorous sculpting, living in a world of imagination that strains to correspond with the world actually based in reality—then and now, true love's definition calls to mind a common one for a person self-obsessed with their many different selves. "Love is a thing full of anxious fear" is how Ovid put it over two thousand years ago and since then little has changed. The only difference is now there are more ways to be anxious, more ways to enact fear in one's heart and mind.

*

One of my own definitions of prudery entails wearing a tightly cinched trench coat while clothed in shorts and t-shirt beneath, standing at the corner of two busy intersecting streets. With great interest and diligence, scrutinizing each passerby, then flashing those found most inviting and alluring. Staring deep into each person's eyes as their mix of reactions flushes through, great cavalcade of emotion from shock to anger to, upon realizing, amused annoyance. Then, focused only on the public beauty of my own private self, scouring past to find and entice the next one.

*

To want attention and affection to such a degree that the more it's received the more it's repudiated and desired. Shameful, true, this is my crucible.

*

More of the King of Love's Rules from *The Art of Courtly Love*:

X. Love is always a stranger in the home of avarice.

XV. Every lover regularly turns pale in the presence of his beloved.

XX. A man in love is always apprehensive.

*

According to a 2017 Center for Disease Control and Prevention (CDC)/National Center for Health Statistics study, the average heterosexual American male (aged 25-44) will have sex with four to eight partners in his lifetime; the same number set holds true for the average heterosexual American female (aged 25-44). Just over 21% of heterosexual American males will have sex with more than fifteen females in their lifetimes and just over 10% of heterosexual American females will have sex with more than fifteen males in their lifetimes. Exotic, depending on the person, in their sparseness or in their abundance, these numbers haven't changed much in the past twenty years. What's changed is the amount of sexual content one comes in contact with over the course of a lifetime.

*

In her book *Love and Limerence: The Experience of Being in Love* (1979), psychologist Dorothy Tennov elucidates what exactly happens between love and lust, lust and romance. According to Tennov, limerence is, at the most basic level, the desire for emotional reciprocation from a love interest or potential love interest. Although the desire for it, of course, plays some role, "[s]ex is neither essential nor, in itself, adequate to satisfy the limerent need." When limerent there is instead acute sensitivity and intensity of feeling. Whether the beloved is receptive, averse or indifferent, the lover is deeply in the throes of their entire person, every way and every whim. Limerence is being forced to live in a constant state of inconstancy, grasping, greedy, without self-will.

*

And it all depends on the individual; no two cases are alike. Everyone is needy while limerent, and for some this manifests itself in flower bouquets or carefully crafted mix tapes, given to the object of one's affection at a well-lit French bistro or outside an independent record store. Attempting to decimate their need, others go on the offensive, hoping to "tie down" (phrasing!) the love interest and thus rid themselves of their limerent grief, its unsureness. Using words like *believe, one* and *everything*, these types are direct. They want to know because, if not, they want to move on.

Still another group deals with their limerence by negotiating a shyness both public and private, near-mute in front of the object of one's desires and while later lying awake in bed, thinking only about that near-muteness. He should know how I feel, she *has* to know how I feel, but outright saying something to the object of one's desire is, of course, impossible. There's the fear of rejection, sure, but also something greater than that, an absolute involving the self and, elsewhere, everyone else. Lovesickness that mazes around and into and back around again, omnipresent but silent.

*

Facts! Data! History! Definitions and redefinitions and anecdotes! All just words, silly and little, masking, masking.

*

Even now I still don't know how to write about L, so I'll describe her bedroom. It was small, ordered. In it there was a sense of frivolity mitigated by a queen-sized bed that sat sentinel in the center of the room like some oblong lump of dissuasion, dirty headboard a solemn shield. Brown comforter, maroon pillowcases enclosing aggressively feather-less pillows, clean white sheets. The bedroom's ceiling and walls were painted a beautiful deep blue, hardwood floor stained with a million past tenants' spills and haste. *I don't really care about the contrasts. Interior decoration is a waste of time* she said to me early in our relationship, as if my questioning of the room's color selection was tantamount to admitting that appearances matter only to fickle people who allow them to matter. They mattered to me.

L was a writer and musician, one interested in critical theory and experimental music. Her desk was covered with neatly organized papers and books. Using the past tense is a cowardly means of allowing myself emotional distance. L is a writer and musician, one interested in critical theory and experimental music.

*

A distinct childhood memory of mine: aged five or six and preparing to cross a street with my father on my right and my mother on my left. "Hold my hand, sweetheart," my mother said. "Hold your mom's hand, honey," my father said. Turning to my mother, I blanched, made a face, then proceeded to put my own right hand in my own left hand, staunch in my independence. "I can do it myself," I hissed.

*

We dated for two and a half years, L and I. I fell in love.

*

With her? Or with my self?

*

"The currency of exchange for most social and moral attitudes is that ancient device of the drama: personifications, masks…the mind sets up these figures, simple and definite, whose identity is easily stated, who arouse quick loves and hates. Masks are a peculiarly effective, shorthand way of defining virtue and vice," writes Susan Sontag in her essay "Going to theatre, etc." They allow us our full spectrum of self, masks do, only some of these veilings are deemed favorably (the passionate lover, full of deserved ardor) or unfavorably (the would-be lover, needy and limerent, helpless unto their desire) by wider society.

One of L's favorite writers was Susan Sontag. She had a postcard of her portrait taped to the corner of her desk.

*

With her. When we started dating I was twenty-four and she was twenty-six. As the singer and lyricist, L also played in a successful, nationally touring band. On certain mornings she played the ukulele badly in bed, her red hair embering in a subtly spectacular way, her green eyes so intently focused on the strings that her cat batting its paw against the window at a squawking bird outside earned no attention or response. L was perfect in a way that taught me how dangerous idealizations such as perfection can be, especially during one's twenties.

*

"Nothing is mysterious, no human relation. Except love," confided Susan Sontag to her journal in 1965. Thirty-five years later, in 2000, Sontag did the math, calculated the mystery in an interview in *The Guardian*: "I love beauty. So what's new?" She says she has been in love seven times in her life, which seems quite a lot. "No, hang on," she says. "Actually, it's nine. Five women, four men."

*

With L my limerence exhibited itself in the aforementioned carefully crafted mix tape nervously given to her outside Nextwave, the best independent record store in our hometown of Boise, Idaho. Email links to hard-to-find art documentaries available only on Vimeo, second date conversation starters beginning with how the longest page on Wikipedia was "List of Noble Laureates by university affiliation," followed by "List of compositions by Franz Schubert, "List of compositions by Johann Sebastian Bach" and "List of Australian treaties." But I was lucky. L was listening, watching, laughing. She also liked the way I thought and smelled.

Not knowing love, however, I was also reckless. And stupid. Proverbial "all I care about is not caring," with a dash of impetuous youth on the side. When you're young, you're young.

*

"I equated sexuality with truth," the writer Rachel Cusk once said of her libidinous 20s. "Inhabiting my body powerfully was the key to it. Sex has always been incredibly interesting to me, and it becomes more so. Which is strange, because my self-consciousness is so extreme."

*

One of my own definitions of prudery entails fucking—fucking girlfriends, fucking boyfriends, fucking spouses and strangers and coworkers and bosses—to mask one's own confusion and insecurity. This is perhaps an antiquated definition of mine, ill-prepared to advance with the times. Nevertheless it feels true prudery as hyper-sexual so as to not have to directly deal with what one actually feels, who one actually is.

*

L onstage at Cee Bar, looking at me but also past into the crowd, her hair a sweaty tangle, bangs stapled to her forehead and the ruddy mass behind it limber and taut, audience members in front and behind me calling out song names, calling out L's name. L telling me, at a nervous third-date dinner, that the key to meeting anyone is simply pretending you already know them, that early on in a relationship intimacy is a ploy that simply needs to be enacted in one's head. *You just imagine and believe and then it comes true.* At a diner, L and I drawing on the virgin-white paper place-setting in front of us, her concentric, animalist shapes and snares eventually meeting my big-footed stick figures in the middle, the roof of their house shared beneath two spiraling steeples. L angrily listening to someone else talk down to her, face a dark static waiting for its own chance to fiercely sound. L reading contemplatively, L on the couch watching TV, L sleeping beside me, dawn, dusk, in and out her breath something I wanted to eat, tangible.

*

"By your side I'm most quiet and most unquiet, most inhibited and most free" being the way Franz Kafka put it to his confidante and probable lover Milena Jesenská shortly before his death. Such is the way I felt while in a relationship with L. Perfectly aligned, each shadow had its corresponding allotment of sun, and as our bodies moved both the dark and the light shone through.

*

The deeper I fell in love with L, though, the more my self-consciousness became an issue. I wondered aloud about futures and separate living situations and why, when L went out on certain nights, she turned her cell phone off. I asked questions that I didn't want the answers to, ones I insisted on asking due to that fact. Proudly independent when I met her, I became meekly so the longer we dated. The more time elapsed the more I silently wished we could just jump from growing up young together to growing old together, without having to deal with the hundreds of important and necessary moments in between. One of L's

·lf became my only version for her, and that entombing became
· mind.

A lifelong bachelor, Kafka was yet engaged three times during the course of his life, twice to the same woman. In the end he never married. Serving as both a source of inspiration and defeat, Kafka's fear of inadequacy (a "disease of the instincts" is how he described the sexual act) was buttressed by his need to have a woman in his life that he loved, one that he could not do without. Stunted desire was thus the source of his artistic genius and erotic insolvency, the two things co-existing to create the successful failure that was Franz Kafka.

*

"Every work of art is a work of perfect necessity" is how one of the characters in William Gaddis's novel *The Recognitions* puts it. For many years, such was my belief also regarding love. Need and necessity, in my opinion, outweighed everything else. What I didn't realize is how flimsy that word sounds—*need, need, need*—when buttressed against other words, words like *listen* and *can't.* Those words, I learned, have a granite-hewn heft.

*

What are you thinking about?

I'm thinking about if you can be in love with someone and not want to be with them she responded, her head on my chest, her feet dangling off the bed beneath me, toes and ankles where I could not see.

*

And yet.

*

XXII. Jealousy, and therefore love, are increased when one suspects his beloved.

XXVIII. A slight presumption causes a lover to suspect his beloved.

XX. A man in love is always apprehensive.

*

Introduced by a mutual friend that, ice-breaking, we each bashfully admitted to not knowing the last name of, L and I slept together the night we met. Both four beers-buzzed, neither sloppy nor sober, but my fumblings still seemed interminable to L. There were feints and there were miscalculations and there were mumblings half-exasperated. At one point L sarcastically asked *Are you a virgin?*, the *you* lilting upwards into territory that seemed dangerous to breach with any type of substantive response.

Afterwards, though, L said she meant it *almost like a compliment... You're shy. But down. It's actually kind of hot.*

*

Taking their name from a piece of graffiti spotted by the lead singer—and not having anything to do with the psychoanalytic concept of the absent father— the lyrics to the pop punk band Daddy Issues' song "I'm Not" read, in part:

If you want
You can read my diary
I've got nothing left to lose
I've been losing since I lost my virginity
Just another pretty face, I'm no use
...

They wouldn't get it sweetheart, please don't tell on me
I let my memories fall through
It's not my fault
I blame my sexuality
I feel promiscuous but maybe I'm a prude

A melodic, fast-paced rock song, "I'm Not" sounds like a lot of other songs in existence. What differentiates it from all those others, then, is lead singer Jenna Moynihan's stark pleading when she sings, over and over, "You're so, you're so great/And I'm not/ I'm not."

*

I wasn't a virgin when L and I first fornicated, although her question didn't offend me either. If anything, it made me feel like one of the select males not part of some toxic masculinity, arrogant or unknowing, that L knew the flubberings of intimately, the (vast) difference between a guy saying one thing in the morning at the coffeeshop and then saying or doing another at the bar that night. How, far from being just seven syllables, a distinctive, albeit meaningless, phrase, the words meant something fanged and true and L had been forced to live in their meaning her whole life.

*

You have really good manners is how L described my sexual nature in an email to me after we'd been dating for a few months. *I like breaking them with you. I like letting you forget.*

*

A year later than most Americans typically do, I was eighteen when I lost my virginity, to K. In late June at her family's empty hillside cabin an hour outside of Boise. What can be said about this pleasurable box-checking other than that it felt like a successful evasion of some kind? We had a few beers to kill the nerves; we had consent and anticipative anxiety. K and I'd been dating for a few months, liked each other a lot and felt prepared to affirm such feelings physically. A short while later then it was done. We were happily conscripted into the sexful adult world.

Although triumphant, the following days and weeks between K and I often felt like a scene from the satirical TV comedy *Flight of the Conchords*, one where the main character Bret, shy but engagingly attractive, sits awkwardly next to his new girlfriend Coco, both debating the merits of the meal they just finished together:

B: The carrots were really nice. And the broccoli was really nice as well.
C: Yeah…it did turn out really nice.
B: Yeah, really nice. It was really nice.
C: Yeah, it was really nice…like your eyes. I could look at them for ages.
B: The eggs were really nice like your lips. So…your lips look delicious like…as

delicious as the eggs. Probably more delicious.
B: Do…do you want to kiss me?
C: (*immediately*) Oh, yes please.

Having done what we wanted to do, K and I still didn't exactly know who we were to one and other or what was next. Such, of course, is youth, and eventually K and I grew apart, fondly moved on, etc., etc. But until I met L I still often lived within Bret and Coco's *Flight of the Conchords* scene framework, wanting without knowing how to articulate it physically or emotionally. Funny and knowledgeable, I went on dates frequently and, after some inevitable shy bumbling on my part, slept with women less frequently, but confusion still reigned supreme inside me, my self a torrent of attributed and unattributed need.

*

"I feel promiscuous but maybe I'm a prude," sings Jenna Moynihan on "I'm Not." It's that *maybe* that holds all interest, the consideration of whether prudery can also be synonymous with promiscuity and the dovetailing of shy with selfish. The pleasure of the forbidden; the open window beside the locked door.

*

In sociologist Eva Illouz's book *Why Love Hurts: A Sociological Explanation* (2012) Illouz writes on the concept of "enchanted love," a concept that she introduces via influential sociologist Max Weber's contention that the prime characterization of modernity is that of disenchantment. To wit:

> "Disenchantment does not mean simply that the world is no longer filled with angels and demons, witches and fairies, but that the very category of "mystery" becomes disparaged and meaningless. For, in their impulse to control the natural and social world, the various modern institutions of science, technology, and the market, which aim at solving human problems, relieving suffering, and increasing well-being, also dissolve our reverence toward nature, our capacity to believe and to keep a sense of mystery…[w]hile romantic love retains a uniquely strong emotional and cultural hold on our desires and fantasies, the cultural scripts and tools available to fashion it have become increasingly at odds with and are even undermining the sphere of the erotic. There are thus at least two cultural structures at work

> in the emotion of love: one based on the powerful fantasy of erotic self-abandonment and emotional fusion; the other based on rational models of emotional self-regulation and optimal choice."

Illouz goes on to enumerate the "elementary forms of '"enchanted"' love as… cultural prototype." Near-mirrors of some of the rules of Capellanus's "King of Love," in total these include:

1. The object of love is sacred.

2. Love is impossible to justify or explain.

3. Such an experience overwhelms the experiential reality of the lover.

4. In enchanted love, there is no distinction between subject and object of love.

5. The object of love is unique and incommensurable.

6. The person in love is oblivious to his or her own self-interest as a criterion for loving another person.

*

Modernity and our modern experience, Illouz states, has rendered the above "enchanted love" rules and notions null and void in their wrinkled, whitebeard obsolescence. As a category of enchantment, mystery isn't enticing so much as tired and overwrought. Nothing is mysterious. Especially not love, its flooded marketplace filled with so many bad or hapless actors.

*

Starring Tom Hanks and Meg Ryan or Will Smith and Eva Mendes or Drew Barrymore and Adam Sandler, L loved romantic comedies with an earnest tenderness that belied all her other aesthetic and analytical pursuits. She refused to accept criticism for this proclivity of hers. In her opinion, the phrase "guilty pleasure" was oxymoronic. *Those words shouldn't exist side by side.*

*

For most of our relationship, L also kept a diary of sorts, a small, non-descript Moleskine notebook with a black cover and no stickers or identifiable markers. It was kept in the bottom drawer of her desk, with her Sontag postcard fortressing the surroundings up top. Originally the diary was begun as a tour travelogue, with both her and her band members contributing. When the tour ended, though, L kept it and kept writing; I'd see it on the nightstand next to her bed or on her kitchen table. I often wondered but never asked, instead resorting to light mocking re: stereotype and cliché— keeping a diary in a Moleskine notebook, changing the world one old-fashioned artisan-papered page at a time.

*

What is the erotic capital of a prude? It depends on the person, their performance of self (sexually; shyly) vis-à-vis their partner's. For the first two years that we dated L and I yinged and yanged like Voltron, swimmingly in sync. Nothing was taught, only learned, and learned often, several times a week, new every time. Although comfort and trust built gradually at the start of our relationship, in bed with L I soon felt at home, forgetting my mind for my body, L's body.

*

In his *The Unquiet Grave* the 20th century British literary critic Cyril Connolly—writing under the pen name Palinurus—remarks:

"A puritan is incomplete because he excludes that half of himself of which he is afraid, and so the deeper he imprisons himself in his fastidiousness, the more difficulty he has in finding a woman who is brave enough to simulate the vulgarity by which he can be released."

*

Fear, fastidiousness, blissful vulgarity. Each state seems to be at odds with the other; each, according to Connolly, needs to be reckoned with in order for a puritan to be made whole. Such transformations cannot be made, however, without the help of another human being. It takes two.

*

L laughing at a bad joke of mine, mouth open, eyes emerald and bright. L pouting in the bathroom mirror while flossing, and, upon seeing me peeking from outside the bathroom, flipping herself off in the mirror at me, exclaiming *I wish I had the courage to be an anti-dentite.* Attempting to flag down a friend on a windy day, L animated outside a coffee shop, her farmer's tan wholly evident via her red tank-top and green skirt pairing, her detachment from this discordance its own singular beauty. Late at night in a crowded bar, The Misfits on in the background, L attempting to explain to me and one of her bandmates the origin of the phrase *the banality of evil*, both its portent and danger. L calling me on the phone and, not waiting for me to say hello, manically exclaiming *Hi. Hi. Let us now try and talk for a day without using contractions. No it's or let's or what's or any of them. There will be much joy if we succeed and much lamentation if we fail. Let us agree to this game posthaste.* L in bed, watching me undress, shyly smiling. Having sex with L and feeling like a concentric shape of some kind, alien to my body but still fully part of it, L and I incapable of further distinction. L stretching in her apartment, sun salutation, the morning's sunlight decadently spraying over the hardwood.

*

L diligent at her desk, crafting ornate wallets out of two rolls of cheap duct tape, gray and black, every one of which will instantly sell at her band's next show, with each buyer expressing amazement at L's DIY artistry. Feet in motion before her arms have the chance to catch up, L walking towards me on an unseasonably warm fall day, mouth agape, eyes shining, pointing behind at me what I don't turn around to look at. At the movies with L and staring at her face in the dark, lovingly confounded by the mystery. Telling L I loved her, hearing her say it in return and at first feeling nothing, an emptiness that strangely didn't bother me. Three days later, then, feeling the full brunt of L's admission when, outside her band's empty practice space, I heard her before I saw her and stood listening to her sing alone with her headphones on; I was living in a bad rom-com and had never been happier. L and I lying happy in her old ugly bed, with her giving a long monologue on the dangers of watching the show *Gilmore Girls* while stoned, my attempts to butt into her soliloquy batted away by L with a high-pitched utterance of *Nuh-uh* until finally we both simultaneously grabbed at the other's waist, ravenous. L scratching her nose, L wiping gunk out of her eyes. L crying at

her sister's wedding and me starting to cry at seeing her tears. L s
dirty and white.

*

From *The Unquiet Grave*, Connolly on love:

> "Is it possible to love any human being without being torn limb from limb? No one was ever made wretched in a brothel; there need be nothing angst-forming about the sexual act. Yet a face seen in the tube can destroy our peace for the rest of the day, and once a mutual attraction develops it is too late; for when sexual emotion increases to passion, then something starts growing which possesses a life of its own and which, easily though it can be destroyed by ignorance and neglect, will die in agony and go on dying after it is dead."

*

I like drawing you out L said more than once. *And then you come and remember.*

*

Connolly was married thrice in his life. Soon after his unexpected death in 1974, his third wife, Deirdre Craven, remarried, to a former voluntarily celibate Jesuit priest.

*

And yet.

*

I fell in love. With L or with my self?

*

With her.

*

With my self, my desire for security. Increasingly jealous, apprehensive of the many known knowns and known unknowns, eventually I forced L into my imagination. Who she was, what she said and did, were all products of my being able to believe in a future that, being the future, was unknowable; it would have be lived instead of predicted. Surreptitiously, I began checking out books from the library by different theorists L liked—Sontag, Foucault, Barthes—in order to understand her ways of thinking better. I went to every show her band played, including those on the road within a 100-mile radius of Boise. I became a professional exhaustor, both to her and my self. After six months of this L broke up with me. While doing so, I accused her of, among other things, being selfish and self-absorbed.

*

In her chapbook *On Imagination* (2017), the poet Mary Ruefle writes, “I have lived with my imagination, and in my imagination, for so long that I have no memory of any time on earth without it. It is my daimon if there ever was one. “‘The daimon is a kind of twin that prowls alongside, is most often vivid when things are tough, that pushes you toward the life you signed up to live before you fell into the amnesia of birth and forgot the whole affair.’”

*

“Is there not perhaps within the heart of a prude a certain lack of courage accompanied by a degree of mean vengefulness?” writes the 19th century French author Stendhal in his seminal book-length essay *On Love* (1822). After *On Love* was published and failed to gain support from either readers or critics, Stendhal wrote three apologetic prefaces, the opening sentence of the first stating, “This book has met with no success; it has been found unintelligible, and not without cause.” He goes on to denounce, among other things, his digressive egotism and self-centeredness, while yet insisting there can be no other way to honestly impart the full breadth of his thoughts. What Stendhal says he sees in the imaginative scope of his mind’s ever-roving eye he must write. He must. There can be no other way.

*

It is wretched and deceiving, living in one’s imagination, in love, selfish for the future while pissing deep into the snow of the present, eating one’s beloved up with misplaced jealousy and passion.

*

One of my own definitions of prudery entails the daimon haunting [illegible] being mistaken for the person living it. For imaginative people, the imagination is selfish, greedy. It breathes; it lives. Vengeful, it racks and exhausts.

*

3. Such an experience overwhelms the experiential reality of the lover.

*

X. Love is always a stranger in the home of avarice.

*

"There are thus at least two cultural structures at work in the emotion of love: one based on the powerful fantasy of erotic self-abandonment and emotional fusion; the other based on rational models of emotional self-regulation and optimal choice" is how Eve Illouz puts it in *Why Love Hurts*. Based on the sustainability of passionate self-deception and the privation of the human will when in the throes of said passion and deception, I would identity at least one more cultural structure in the work of emotion of love.

*

Words, they're all just.

*

The breakup hurt. The breakup hurt. And where, after two and a half years, I wanted assurance and security, no matter the cost, L—wiser and older— desired something different. As cliché as it is, which it is, which means little, words lack, weak thimblefuls of water beside feeling's oceanic rumblings, fathoms deep, L wanted to be her own variegated self rather than the concrete, unalterable vision of her that I possessed. She wanted to accrue romantic and erotic capital anew.

*

"My angel, my all, my own self" is how Beethoven put it in his 1812 "Immortal Beloved" letter, writing to an unidentified lover widely believed to be Countess Josephine Brunsvik. In achieving the lover's own being, though, something is lost, something mysterious and unknown.

*

Soon after our dissolution, L started dating a fellow musician, older than her by a considerable number of years. Eleven years later, their relationship continues to this day.

*

Mysterious, unknown and impossible. Beethoven never married and, although in love with him also, Countess Brunsvik cut off their involvement in 1807, choosing in 1810 to instead marry within her aristocratic class-set, to the Estonian baron Christoph von Stackelberg. The marriage was a profoundly unhappy one. For his part, Beethoven died alone.

*

After L and I parted ways, I thought a great deal about sex, adequacy and family. I thought about naturality and normality and social construction, about the dominant expectations of desire. About the difference between shyness and selfishness, if there was a difference, if it mattered. From Calhouna St. in Bellingham, WA, I moved apartments and towns, entered my first graduate school. Framing my worldly outlook through books, I began to read more widely.

*

In his much-quoted and cited 1914 paper "On Narcissism," Sigmund Freud writes, "The charm of a child lies to a great extent in his narcissism, his self-contentment and inaccessibility, just as does the charm of certain animals which seem not to concern themselves about us, such as cats and large birds of prey."

*

How, if not actively wrong and imprecise, Freud is endlessly reaching. In her book *In the Freud Archives* (1984), Janet Malcolm records the myriad petty squabbles between a group of seminal late 20th century Freudian psychoanalysts and former Freudian psychoanalysts. Early in the text Malcolm declares, "To fully accept the idea of unconscious motivation is to cease to be human…The crowning paradox of psychoanalysis is the near-uselessness of its insights." I can't help but agree with her.

*

Look, I know about The Oedipus complex and crisis, know about castration anxiety. How, to become a societal-sanctioned "man," the mother must be left behind so as to contend with the father. But I don't exist in what I can't be bothered about. Beyond accepting that ambiguity and not knowing is forever tantalizing, I don't believe.

*

I believe in the certainty of release and a pure swath of liminality that makes up one's life entire. I believe in anxiety and indeterminacy, in understanding when a surface or sensation seems securely supportable or when its main quality seems to be nebulous flimsiness. No matter the definition, I believe in honesty, love and hope, believe in a willful suspension of disbelief.

*

In *Intimacies*, his co-authored book with the psychoanalyst Adam Phillips, theorist Leo Bersani provides a counterpoint: "...we may judge the great achievement of psychoanalysis to be its attempt to account for our inability to love others and ourselves. The promises of adaptive balance and sexual maturity undoubtedly explain the appeal of psychoanalysis as therapy, but its greatness may lie in its insistence on a human destructiveness resistant to any therapeutic endeavors whatsoever."

*

"We are all haunted houses" writes H.D. in her volume *Tribute to Freud* (1956). Walls of each room alternately smudged or pristine, floor beams constantly creaking or eerily tenacious with grip, this assertion of H.D.'s I believe in. But I don't need Freud and his theories to get there.

*

And yet.

*

Discussing Freud's "On Narcissism" in "The Bad Boyfriend" chapter of her book *The Selfishness of Others: An Essay on the Fear of Narcissism* (2016), Kristin Dombek writes:

> “When we grow up and learn to love, we forfeit a part of this early childhood narcissism—impoverishing our oceanic, boundless self-absorption in order to care and be cared about. Genuinely loving parents teach their children it is safe to make this trade. But if a child turns outward from the natural megalomania of the toddler years to seek and give love and finds her parents cold, cruel, or violent, there is nothing to affirm her tender efforts. So she reverses course, veers inward, and attaches her searching affection to her own little ego, to be safe, retaining into adulthood the “omnipotence of thoughts” of early childhood. Narcissism is, in this sense, the sexual version of the instinct to self-preservation.

*

I'm selfish for my self but only in relation to my estimation of what the world, that mob-mentality of purported adulthood, lacks.

*

Securely married for 30+ years, my parents were and are uncold, uncruel and unviolent. They were present and engaged while raising me. If physical affection—hugging, affectionate caressing—was occasionally absent, love in the form of emotional support and encouragement was, no matter the situation, always steadfastly there. They believed in the best version of me, even if that version was not one that they fully understood. (Nor one that I fully understood.)

*

What wasn't discussed in my household growing up: sex. Talking about it would have been like talking about the (invisible) oxygen in the (invisible) air—if its importance could not be overstated, it could also not be worth parsing out the unseen particulars. Like cats and large birds of prey, air seems to not concern itself with us. Thus we all learn to breathe at our own pace, even if a throw in the deep soon accelerates things.

What wasn't discussed in my household growing up: any concept of the healthy non-adolescent self. Their own parents having been caring, albeit fitfully so, my parents didn't coddle or helicopter me. They instead assumed that, same as them, selfhood and where each successful version of it slots in—from the romantic to the professional to the sexual—would eventually come together for me. Stops and starts and stops once more, this assumption proved correct and less than so.

*

"The greatest man is the one who is the most incoherent," ordains Fernanda Pessoa by way of the heteronym Álvaro de Campos.

*

"The more active your sensitivity, the more the needle of repentance will torment you," writes the Marquis de Sade in his novel *Justine*, or the *Misfortunes of Virtue* (1791).

*

In the two years following my breakup with L I copulated with thirteen different women, seeing none of them for longer than five months. Egotistical, disenchanted, yet also acutely sensitive to I knew not what or whom, I came around to the belief that sex and, if it was bumbled into, love were profoundly unimportant, simply fatalistic means to already established ends.

*

A lurid, darkly unsentimental coming-of-age story involving sex, AIDS, skateboarding and teenaged youth, set in New York in the early 1990's and released in 1995 to widespread notoriety, a scene from the script of the NC-17 rated film *Kids*:

INT. PAUL'S APARTMENT - DAY

Some of the guys are sitting in front of the couch doing whip-its. Casper is chewing on a microwave burrito and watching the guy next to him play Nintendo. He is blowing into the burrito.

They are in the midst of a conversation.

STANLEY
Yeah, yeah, yeah!

PAUL
That's the one thing. They expect you to be so gentle, so kind...

ZACK
When most of time you just wanna be all. Pounding on that shit.

STANLEY
That would be the best if you could just be. Excuse me can I borrow your hole Miss? It'll only take a little while. I'll give it right back.

Laughter.

TELLY
But that's the thing. Girl's like it slow. They like romance. They like things to be sweet and romantic.

CASPER
Yep.

TELLY
I mean I've been with a lot of girls I know.

CASPER
Yeah me too.

*

Referencing the prudishness of the current era, "It would be impossible to make that film now" is how Harmony Korine, the writer of *Kids*, put it in 2015. "You could never get away with it."

*

All the characters in *Kids* only care about themselves. They are inaccessible, self-contained and narcissistic. But they're kids. When you're young, you're young.

*

L introduced me to *Kids*, which she owned on DVD. It wasn't one of her favorite movies, but she watched it least once a year in order to remember *what it's like to be alive like that, where nostalgia and regret don't exist, it's all eternal and eternal.*

*

Entails an attempt to extinguish the past by relentlessly existing in the present, no matter the personal or emotional cost, one of my own definitions of prudery. Prudently bearing witness to the child forever in one's heart, allowing it a yawp of exclamation, triumphant. Some form of sexual self-preservation as a way of pleading that there is, in fact, some semblance of self to preserve.

*

R.

*

Sleeping with R made clear to me how existing outside of hookup culture does not mean that while you are passionately, tenderly making love to your partner or spouse or significant other, the one, the only, you are not also baldly hooking up, animalistic, with said partner or spouse or significant other. No matter how romantic, affirming or love-suffused, genital-unions are just that.

*

R. Unlike with L, writing about R I can do with my eyes closed, hands tied behind my back.

*

Via the wildness that is the World Wide Web is how I met her. She was studying dance at a local university while also waiting tables on the side. Online, we bonded over our love of reading (*what's the point if it's not weird?!* R wrote in one of her first messages to me) and our mutual desire to, when the time was right, own aquariums housing dozens of happy, compatible fish, each swimming peacefully against the greeny-filtered-blue, trapped content in their ignorance. Both R and I were twenty-seven when we met.

*

In the "Internet Dating" section of her essay collection *Future Sex* (2016), Emily Witt, at the time having just turned thirty, discusses her nervousness vis-à-vis finding a sexual partner online, stating:

> "My timidity not only concerned ideas of sexual "safety" … My avoidance of sex also had a lot to do with an equation, a relationship of exchange around which I organized my ideas. I saw sex as a lever that moderated climatic conditions within the chamber of life, with a negative correlation between the number of people I slept with and the likelihood of encountering love. Being sexually cautious meant I was looking for "something serious." Having sex with more people meant I privileged the whims of the instant over transcendent higher-order commitments that developed over long stretches of time. I equated promiscuity with youth culture and thought of longer monogamous relationships as more adult, and it seemed depressing to still be having casual sex on a regular basis for an interminable number of years. The arbitrary nature of these correlations had not occurred to me."

*

Even though I'd had it with other partners before I met her, while dating L I had been under the youthful impression that sex was something recently discovered by us and only us, that all the whisperings and shouts of it everywhere else in the world were, in fact, decoys or meandering diversions from the actual, that thing that only L and I knew. "I have found the secret/ Of loving you/Always for the first time" in André Breton's words.

Maudlin and sentimental, this belief of mine.

And true.

*

Sleeping with R was the equivalent of jumping into a cold shower after pruning for hours in a hot bath. It takes a few minutes to wake up.

*

But so many I's and so many first times, in and out and again. Secrets upon secrets. Poets imagine what the world ignores.

*

We screwed frequently and infrequently, R and I, communicating on a sporadic text-based basis. Whereas L had taken my sexual shyness as a positive attribute, something to enjoyably maneuver within, R liked to, alternately, be in control or be controlled, the sheer justness of her lust an all-conquering and dominating force. Like Witt, I'd always assumed, without ever truly thinking about it, that "[b]eing sexually cautious meant I was looking for "something serious," that "[h]aving sex with more people meant I privileged the whims of the instant over transcendent higher-order commitments that developed over long stretches of time."

There would be others, but R was the first to glean a crack of light on the idea that sex is a romance with the self, *your* self and its ecstasy, and allowing one's partner to have too much say in the matter will only produce snobbish, self-conscious sex. R was the first partner of mine to insist that we fuck in public at a zoo, if only because even the thought—let alone the actuality— of doing so made me immensely uncomfortable.

*

I've never met a guy like you... you're repressed! Hot and repressed! R texted me more than once.

*

Takes a few minutes to wake up and then you're glad you did. Love is a sleepwalking down the same corridor at the same time of night every night. Life is meant to be lived while awake.

*

Own your lecherous self, own your selfishness.

*

`Excuse me can I borrow your hole Miss? Can I borrow your thrust, your stupid little chub Sir? It'll only take a little while. I'll give it right back.`

*

R was also the first to introduce me to the tactics of the Pickup Artist, that rare breed of pleasure dome decree. For R the fact that those strategies were gendered, conceived as a means of covert male coercion and domination, meant no difference. She was fascinated and admitted she'd used a few of the tactics on me when we'd first met. A sculptor works with the materials at hands, massaging and molding them into what she will, when she will. Where the coarse rock comes from matters only as much as the sculptor lets it.

*

Four months after we started hooking up, R embarked on a cross-country summer road trip and I never saw her again. I think of her now with the greatest fondness.

*

Perhaps the best version of me is one that relishes fucking in public at zoos, unabashedly staring into the cages and pseudo-wildlife preserves, animal to animal, one and the same.

*

And yet.

*

In his *The History of Sexuality—Volume I: An Introduction* (1976), Michel Foucault talks at great length about the nature of sexual repression, which he views as confused and contradictory. The common view is that "modern sexual repression" began its ascent in the 17th century and continues, albeit in a somewhat lessened state, to this day. "By placing the advent of the age of repression in the seventeenth century, after hundreds of years of open spaces and free expression, one adjusts it to coincide with the development: it becomes an integral part of the bourgeois order."

*

Thus my prudery wasn't—isn't— even mine. Instead it's merely part of the larger collective culture, the indoctrinated bourgeois order I was born into. Cog in the machine.

*

Foucault, however, takes issue with this stereotypical view, asserting that "when one looks back over these last three centuries with their continual transformations, things appear in a very different light: around and apropos of sex, one sees a veritable discursive explosion."

This explosion, however involved its own controlled policing, specifically over rhetoric, allusion, metaphor and statement. In "The Repressive Hypothesis," Part Two of *The History of Sexuality—Vol. I*, Foucault imparts:

> "A control over [sexual] enunciations as well: where and when it was not possible to talk about such things became much more strictly defined; in which circumstances, among which speakers, and within which social relationships. Areas were thus established, if not of utter silence, at least of tact and discretion: between parents and children, for instance, or teachers and pupils, or masters and domestic servants."

*

Silence is quiet, but it was not always that way. Once it was heard in thin rivulets of sound, each a jostling, sexual, social.

*

Foucault believes that beginning in the 17th century and continuing on into the ostensibly sex-cold Victorian era, though, "[t]here was a steady proliferation of discourses concerned with sex—specific discourses, different from one and another both by their form and by their object: a discursive ferment that gathered momentum from the eighteenth century onward…[most] important was the multiplication of discourses concerning sex in the field of exercise of power itself: an institutional incitement to speak about it, and to do so more and more; a determination on the part of the agencies of power to hear it spoken about, and to cause *it* to speak through explicit articulation and endlessly accumulated detail."

*

Thus my prudery wasn't—isn't—even mine. Instead it's a discourse unto a larger power play, one that it is my corporeal duty to discuss and articulate. It's not a choice. It is an obligation of the self in active society.

*

And yet.

*

Suddenly I fear I have not shown myself clearly, with any depth. Addicts often talk about the concept of "terminal uniqueness;" the very dangerous belief that no one has ever faced what you yourself are facing. Growing up I, internally and unknowingly, insisted on such a concept of terminal uniqueness for my self, if for what quality of mine I wasn't at all sure. But I was shy, was selfish, and needed to believe that whatever *it* was, it wasn't a product of my background or my parents or my education or friends or all the rest–it was purely my self, my unique self.

*

"I have seen nothing more weird or miraculous than myself. Over time we get used to strange things, but the more I probe myself and know myself the more my oddity astonishes me and the less I understand who I am," declares Michel de Montaigne in his *Essays*.

*

This is ordinary foolishness, of course. We're all indispensable and unknowable; entirely exclusive, one of a kind. We're all going to make it, and we're all going to make it on our terms, solely based on our unique drive, vision and talent.

*

Nervously losing my virginity at the age of eighteen to K was standard, perfunctory, an ordinary act. As both a teenager and adult, I was neither unsexualized nor aggressively sexualized. (Nor was I asexual in any way. If I was shy, tentative and desirous of security, I also liked to fuck.) Married (to L; to someone else) at twenty-eight or twenty-nine and a subsequent life of writing purely acceptable poems and essays while working or teaching somewhere relatively quiet, no fuss. Eventually starting a family, getting a divorce or both of those things, immersion in the mindfully thoughtless and busy routine of white middle-class happiness, white middle-class indifference, white middle-class drudgery and joy—that life could have easily been me. It all still might. But now only partially do my words match my mind.

*

What I mean to say is that, then or now, if I was ever adept, talented or aware of anything it was with a certain chastity, a certain denial. A detachment that, in the moment, her body right there, available, desire's mutual first time-ness, eternal, I still can't wholly distance my self from. I know I am not unique in this wavering, not at all. Thousands of people experience it daily. Ignoring that fact, though, or choosing not to believe it, gives my life all purpose.

*

"Love is a thing full of anxious fear," especially when what you ultimately love and fear is your self, no matter the cost.

*

A distinct childhood memory of mine: being asked to stay after the period was over in English class, junior year of high school. My teacher, Mrs. S, questioning why my mood and overall demeanor in her class was so sulky, so defiantly high schoolish. "You're smart. You're funny. You're good looking. You have a big friend group. I'm wondering why your attitude in my class doesn't match up to any of those things." I didn't respond, couldn't. When I got a B+ in Mrs. S's class I wasn't surprised. But I felt like I deserved either an A+ or an F.

*

Terminal uniqueness. "I have found the secret…Always for the first time." But has everyone else found it also? And if so, which matters more—the secrecy or the knowledge encased within the secret?

*

"Most people mistake their sexual preferences for a universal system that will or should work for everyone," states cultural anthropologist Gayle Rubin in her landmark 1984 essay "Thinking Sex." Or simply "[p]eople are different from each other," the first of theorist Eve Kosofsky Sedgwick's seven axioms in her 1990 book *Epistemology of the Closet.* People are different from each other and their sexuality identities and proclivities refuse to be organized into unitary cut and dry categories, no matter how hard greater society might wish that were the case. There is no normative sexual citizen; there is no right or wrong way to inhabit and exhibit one's sense of self. Sexual mists swirling in ten thousand and one configurations everywhere around us. But is it possible to go back in time? To be aware then as I am now that sex should not be a source of rumination and mental anguish as much as one of enjoyment and freedom? (O the horror, the shame, the horror.)

*

And yet.

*

Before we parted ways, R recommended three books to me: *The Lover* by Marguerite Duras, *The Box Man* by Kobo Abe and *The Game: Penetrating the Secret Society of Pickup Artists* by Neil Strauss.

*

Autobiographical, loosely based on events in the author's own life, Duras's *The Lover* (1984) assembles the dilemma of its nameless protagonist, a fifteen-year-old white girl living in Southern Vietnam, the product of a broken family, in love with a twenty-seven-year-old Chinese man who is the heir to a substantial fortune.

*

I think you'll like it because it's sad and keeps jumping around is what R texted in her endorsement of the book to me.

*

It's never solved, the dilemma in *The Lover*. No matter her young age, death occurs everywhere around the protagonist—to her troubled father, her abusive mother, her troubled brother—and in the end her lover leaves her for the Chinese woman his father had picked out for him years prior. Regarding love, the book has little new to say; typical eternities and forevers and sorrowful partings, each molded by a loss that seems inevitable before the novel's two main characters even meet. The last sentences of the book read: "And then he told her. Told her that it was as before, that he still loved her, he could never stop loving her, that he'd love her until death."

*

Immortal Beloved. To Fall in Love With Anyone, Do This. Perfect necessity. Enchanted. Enchantment.

*

XIV. The easy attainment of love makes it of little value; difficulty of attainment makes it prized.

*

2. Love is impossible to justify or explain.
5. The object of love is unique and incommensurable.

*

Recalling the book now, years later, I don't remember *The Lover* at all but for its oblique sadness. R was right. Early in, Duras writes, "The story of my life doesn't exist. Does not exist. There's never any center to it. No path, no line. There are great spaces where you pretend there used to be someone, but it's not true, there was no one." decrees Marguerite Duras in The Lover.

*

No path, no line. Over the course of those two years after parting from L, I can recall the names of the women I spent time with, can vividly recall their faces and movements. But hand-in-hand with such recollections is a certain muted emptiness that can also be found in *The Lover*. When pressed on the specifics of the actual vs. the imagined in the book, Duras refused to budge: it was all actual, it was all imagined. "It's in the imaginative memory of time that it is rendered into life" is how she put it.

*

"I have lived with my imagination, and in my imagination, for so long that I have no memory of any time on earth without it. It is my daimon if there ever was one" imparts Mary Ruefle in *On Imagination*. What happened isn't what happened. Nor is it not what happened. It is simply the way we live and, in living, remember.

*

As Duras asserts in *The Lover*, "…it often seems that writing is nothing at all. Sometimes I realize that if writing isn't all things, all contraries confounded, a quest for vanity and void, it's nothing. That if it's not, each time, all things confounded into one through some inexpressible essence, then writing is nothing…"

The Lover was published when its author was seventy, fifty-five years after the events in it were purported to have taken place. When asked why she waited so long to write about the affair, Duras used words like loneliness, truth and desire, interchanging the three words, inextricably conflating them.

*

XXVI. Love can deny nothing to love.

*

"Perhaps / The truth depends on a walk around a lake, // A composing as the body tires…" being how Wallace Stevens describes it in his poem "Notes Toward a Supreme Fiction."

*

Round, straight, the lake keeps growing and growing. I'm still walking, still trying to catch up.

*

Living separate existences in his mind and body, Wallace Stevens's personal life was an utter failure, his marriage to Elsie Kachel strained and loveless, separate bedrooms, separate schedules and social lives, the long nine yards of dysfunction. Thy daimon is thyself.

*

Poet of the imagination, *The Collected Poems of Wallace Stevens* reveals that the poet did not use the word "love" in the titles of any of his poems, not a once. In the beginning to his "Men Made Out of Words," Stevens writes:

What should we be without the sexual myth,
The human revery or poem of death?

Castratos of moon-mash—Life consists
Of propositions about life. The human

Revery is a solitude in which
We compose these propositions, torn by dreams,

By the terrible incantations of defeats
And by the fear that defeats and dreams are one.

*

"A composing as the body tires..." Tiredness beckons but only as far as the water keeps glistening, its beauty a different truth with every ripple.

*

It's perfect for you! It's funny and weird. And he lives in a cardboard box. My sister loved it is what R texted in her recommendation of *The Box Man* to me.

*

He does live in a cardboard box. Epitomizing the concept of the "unreliable narrator," Kobo Abe's *The Box Man* (1974) relates the tale of a nameless man who, due to his desire to see without being seen, to embody all his many different selves at the same exact time, as one, chooses to live in a mobile cardboard box. Haunting the town of T, the slit the box man makes in the front of his box in order to see out is "comparable, as it were, to the expression of the eyes…[t]he worst threatening glare is not so offensive as this slit." The box man aims not to frighten others, however. Instead, he endeavors to contain himself and, in doing so, understand why he needs to be encased in the box at all. The more confined the more comfortable for the box man, and this comfort activates all modes of dreamscape in him, from the nightmarish to the blissful.

*

In frightful love and frightful lust, Abe's box man is a puritan of the first order, a "specialized voyeur" that wants to do more than watch but cannot allow himself the latitude to do so; that would be akin to giving in without a fight. It would be too easy. When he falls in love with a beautiful nurse the box man does what any box man would do—he embraces the situation by waddling away from it, box as shield, his heart plump and full inside of it.

*

("Sexuality will never change, for people have been fucking their own particular ways since time began and will continue to do it. Just more of those ways will be coming to light. It might even reach a puritan state." Thus saith David Bowie in a 1974 *Rolling Stone* interview with William Burroughs. And how that multivalent light can scald and solder and shimmer, its illuminative properties a source of elated restlessness.)

*

The Box Man was not a book I particularly enjoyed reading. Its 178 pages took me long cavernous miles to get through and when I texted R as much she responded with an image of a folded-up cardboard box, followed by a link to the latest ULINE catalog.

*

I think of R now with the greatest fondness.

*

Abe's book, though, taught me, especially at that age, twenty-seven, more than I wanted to know about my self and selves. His world aflutter towards the end of the text, in love, très confused, the box man states, "Instead of leaving the box, I shall enclose the world within it." Since reading it this statement by the box man has never left my mind.

*

Earlier in the volume, two other proclamations made by the box man also forced me awake, if only because they encapsulated what I felt when R ribbed me about my hesitation in terms of fucking with all the lights on and the windows open, mid-afternoon, or, one unseasonably warm spring night, filming it because *why not? No one is going to see it except us:*

"The reason the world ignores box men is because nobody understands who's inside the box."

"It's a paradoxical love, beginning at the end…a love that commences from the realization that it is lost. A poet said it well. It is beautiful to love, but ugly to be loved."

*

XX. A man in love is always apprehensive.

*

R and I were not in love.

*

Doesn't matter.

*

Nobody understands the box man and his solution to this errancy is to, within his confinement, be as many different people as possible as often as possible. Lover, villain, victim, perpetrator, prince, pauper. He (shyly) listens while (aggressively) mansplaining; he is loud and deaf, blind and boorishly drunk. One of the sections of *The Box Man* is entitled "In Which It Is a Question of the Sullen Relationship Between the I Who Am Writing and the I Who Am Being Written About" and, saying too much and not enough, that about says it.

*

Entails trying too hard but, constantly stuck in one's head, not being able to stop, one of my own definitions of prudery. Persistence as failure unending, voracious.

*

From heart failure, Kobo Abe died in Tokyo on January 22nd, 1993. In *The New York Times* his obituary ("Kobo Abe, 68, the Skeptical Poet Of an Uprooted Society, Is Dead") read, in part, "His was a threatening world of people who frequently lose their way and lose their identities, fighting against always insurmountable odds to unravel the senseless events that have left them doomed…At the heart of his art, ultimately, was what some critics described as a pervasive loneliness, as his characters searched for their real and spiritual homes in an inhospitable world."

*

Stop.

*

I never read *The Game: Penetrating the Secret Society of Pickup Artists* (2005) by Neil Strauss.

*

Review of *The Game: Penetrating the Secret Society of Pickup Artists* by R:

It's too beautiful here…I think I'm actually going to stay until next Tuesday, but let's definitely link up when I'm back. And sorry I didn't respond last week… The Game is a complete bullshit book, yeah, but here's what I got out of it—it's at least about realizing the exploitation and intention and accepting it and then eventually living it out in the open. Think about if a woman had written that instead of a man. It'd still be gross and the bullshit that it is but it'd also be downlow like a major feminist statement. In a total "screw it" way kinda. IDK

*

In his essay “Love in the Age of the Pickup Artist” the writer S.
at length, about *The Game*, relating how he lost his first love due to
and overbearingness, both tendencies decidedly non-pickup artist in natu
Belknap goes into the specifics of the pickup artist’s lingo (“false time constraints,” “Demonstrate Value,” “Disarm the Obstacles,” etc.) and overall modus operandi, stating:

> “[T]he message of the pickup artists is at its core an age-old one: women love men who are mean to them—or at least a little mean to them. If you believe that women want to be flattered, wooed and obeyed, we are told, guess again. Women want limits to be set, they want to be played with, they want manliness—and it is best to establish the dynamic right from the start.”

*

Belknap complicates this age-oldness by relating the life, work and theories of the aforementioned 19th century French writer Stendhal, he of a myriad different theories on love, many of them in (subtle or stark) conflict with one and other, and all contained in his volume *On Love* (1822).

For Stendhal there are, in descending order of importance, four different types of love: *vanity-love* (I think they’re hot because my best friend does, because everyone else does), *physical love* (the sex is amazing, regular and urge-filled animalistic), *mannered love* (based on societal norm and decorum and largely devoid of imagination; as Stendhal writes, “A man of breeding will know in advance all the rituals he must meet and observe in the various stages of this kind of love…there is nothing… unpredictable about it”) and *passionate love* (a culmination of all three previous types, but also more than that, deeper, irregular, never before invented or foreseen), with the latter type being, according to Stendhal, the highest of highs. Experiencing it, one becomes immersed in crystallization, the process whereby a lover loves through *imagination* and not reality. From one lover to another, every physical and emotional imperfection is still seen and felt, but it’s the taxonomic categorization there that’s the true problem. Words aren’t feelings, thoughts aren’t feelings, and, no matter their ardor, feelings—emotional, sexual or otherwise—aren’t enough. Fully crystalized in passionate love, every lover doesn’t just believe e lie that the object of one's love has no flaws, will never have any flaws. He or she becomes the lie themselves.

Breaking down the different types of love, Stendhal writes, "What I have called crystallization is a mental process which draws from everything that happens new proofs of the perfection of the loved one." Predicated on the thoroughness of one's imagination, needing it to be relentlessly robust, passionate love is the hardest type to maintain. One minute it's all you know and all you will ever know; a week, month or year later, you can't fathom how you lied to yourself the way you did. Ad infinitum, the mind plays tricks, and the scraps left over are what's often called the self.

*

New proofs of the perfection of the loved one.

*

True eternal love.

*

Based on the thirty-six "closeness-generating procedure" questions in Arthur Aron's paper "The Experimental Generation of Interpersonal Closeness…" (those thirty-six questions "not created…to help [anyone] fall in love,") Mandy Len Catron's *Modern Love* essay "To Fall in Love With Anyone, Do This"—which is predicated on the author's asking of the thirty-six questions (and vice-versa) to a romantic interest that she eventually falls in love with— states near its end:

> "It's true you can't choose who loves you, although I've spent years hoping otherwise, and you can't create romantic feelings based on convenience alone. Science tells us biology matters; our pheromones and hormones do a lot of work behind the scenes.
>
> "But despite all this, I've begun to think love is a more pliable thing than we make it out to be. Arthur Aron's study taught me that it's possible — simple, even — to generate trust and intimacy, the feelings love needs to thrive…
>
> "Love didn't happen to us. We're in love because we each made the choice to be."

To a point, Stendhal and his crystallization theory agree with Catron; love is a choice, one filled with pliability and hormones and pheromones. But, unknowable, unforeseeable, the imagination overrides all of those things according to Stendhal. It lies to us, deceives us. In achieving true eternal love, though, it is our only hope.

*

"The closer I come to you/ In reality/The more does the key sing in the door of the unknown room…Hopeless fusion of your presence and your absence…" decrees André Breton in "Always For the First Time." So Stendhal believes as well: what's impossible to apprehend is far more important than what is readily knowable.

*

In "Love in the Age of the Pickup Artist" Belknap considers a middle ground, one somewhere between pickup artistry, crystallization and scientific biology. Taking his lead from Stendhal's assertion that the "whole art of loving seems to me, in a nutshell, to consist in saying precisely what the degree of intoxication requires at any given moment," Belknap posits that the 21st century lover should be negatively capable, both in the thing and away from it. Being passionately in love all the time is its own deception, and living full-bore, 24-7, in one's head will soon cause it to burst. Refusing too much emphasis on any single aspect of itself, love is a balancing act of intoxications. The adept lover, both passionate and not, intuits this. To wit:

> "The lover should take his cue from Stendhal. The balancing act called for must be duplicated at every level and at every moment: always a genuine passion, and always a compensating restraint. If the lover is truly in love, he will be bursting to ask, bursting to tell, bursting to know and to make known. But he must always be patient, always willing to bide his time, to keep his sweet sentiments and his ardent gestures to himself until the time for them arrives. And though the beloved may waver in her affection, the lover cannot let his faith be shaken. Like Stendhal's ideal conversation with its moments of preparation and moments of naturalness, the love affair as a whole contains moments of distance and moments of closeness; the lover must always adapt, stay ready, and roll with the punches."

*

XXIX. A man who is vexed by too much passion usually does not love.

*

6. The person in love is oblivious to his or her own self-interest as a criterion for loving another person.

*

L. Not wanting to, I think of her. I think of what she might say about all of this, about any of it.

*

Sleeping with fewer people and not beginning to do so until later in their lives, waiting to get married and have children, perhaps Millennials are the poster generation for Belknap's balancing act. It's a taut wire, personal security and assurance, the desire for it. No guarantees. On tiptoe, hands stretched out for support, we walk.

*

"Art is not difficult because it wishes to be difficult, but because it wishes to be art" writes Donald Barthelme in his essay "Not-Knowing." Barthelme posits this statement apropos of discussing how when serious artists are creating new work they often have no idea what they are doing or to what end. "The not-knowing is crucial to art, is what permits art to be made. Without the scanning process engendered by not-knowing, without the possibility of having the mind move in unanticipated directions, there would be no invention" is the way Barthelme's mind congeals on the page.

*

Such is what L would say. That in the two words "pickup artist" the art is being left deep in the dust by the pickup. She would say unknowing is the point, the crucialness, and, with all their premeditated false time constraints and Value Demonstrations, this is something that the pickup artist—a person bad at art—forgets or ignores.

*

And yet.

*

Although "[a]t the height of his "gaming" activity [Neil Strauss] had eight steady sexual partners—who all knew about each other—and was maneuvering himself into threesomes on a regular basis," by the end of *The Game: Penetrating the Secret Society of Pickup Artists* Strauss has acknowledged the fact that "to win the game is to leave it" and is in a happily monogamous relationship. Ten years after *The Game*'s publication, however, in what a cynical observer might call an easily foreseen turn of events, Strauss published *The Truth: An Eye-Opening Odyssey Through Love Addiction, Sex Addiction, and Extraordinary Relationships.* In the book's first section, "Infidelity," Strauss agonizes over cheating on his girlfriend Ingrid (a different girlfriend than Lisa, the one he had contentedly arrived at by the end of *The Game*) before going on to state:

> "We expect love to last forever. Yet as many as 50 percent of marriages and even more remarriages end in divorce. Among those who are married, only 38 percent actually describe themselves as happy in that state. And 90 percent of couples report a decrease in marital satisfaction after having their first child. Speaking of which, more than 3 percent of babies are not actually fathered by the male parent who thinks he did."

*

The mind plays tricks on itself in a game the body keeps forgetting the rules to, no matter one's age, sexuality or relationship status.

*

In the end, anyway, Strauss and Ingrid stay together, at least for the duration of the book. They're in love. They work through it, get married, have a child. Their marriage lasts just over five years.

*

XIX. If love diminishes, it quickly fails and rarely revives.

*

I never read *The Game: Penetrating the Secret Society of Pickup Artists.* But after being dumped by L, and, over the course of two years, sleeping with J and A and C and R and K and P and M and D and T and (a different) C and (a different) D and (a different) T and (a different) A, I felt callow and disenchanted, lacking in all positive imaginative outlets. Self less, selfish. No matter how flawlessly it contoured to my face, I wore a mask that felt like I was wearing a mask. "Sex in one place. Feeling in another," writes Leonard Michaels in his book *Shuffle* (1991). And I could relate.

*

"But vanity, not love, has been my folly," imparts Elizabeth Bennet in Jane Austen's *Pride and Prejudice.*

*

"One is perhaps not made for a single self. One is wrong to cling to this. One takes unity for granted. (Here, as elsewhere, it is our will that impoverishes us, sacrifices us.)

. . .

One wants too much to be someone.

There is no single self. *There are not ten selves. There is no self. SELF is but a point of equilibrium.* (One among a thousand others, always possible, always at the ready.)"

Or so contends the Belgian poet Henri Michaux in his all-over-the-place book-length poem A *Certain Plume.* Michaux's Plume is alternately hero and villain, assertive and timid within the very same instant. Who he is is entirely determined by what he believes he does or does not feel. And round and round we go, back and forth. Where we end is how we begin.

*

"My dirty secret has always been that it's of course about me. But…I'm desperate to unburden my self of my self so I'm coming from nowhere and returning," imparts Eileen Myles in their essay "Long and Social."

*

"But what is the self? The self is a relation that relates itself to itself or is the relation's relating itself to itself in the relation; the self is not the relation but is the relation's relating itself to itself. A human being is a synthesis of the infinite and the finite, of the temporal and the eternal, of freedom and necessity, in short, a synthesis. A synthesis is a relation between two. Considered in this way a human being is still not a self... In the relation between two, the relation is the third as a negative unity, and the two relate to the relation and in the relation to the relation; thus under the qualification of the psychical the relation between the psychical and the physical is a relation. If, however, the relation relates itself to itself, this relation is the positive third, and this is the self."

As averred by Kierkegaard in his book *The Sickness unto Death* (1849), we're all coming from nowhere and returning, our selves forever in flux. Despair is the sole thing that ties all human experience together.

*

In the essay "The artist as exemplary sufferer" Susan Sontag discusses the diaries of the Italian author Cesare Pavese, who committed suicide in 1950. Sontag writes:

> "The diaries are in effect a long series of self-assessments and self-interrogations...Apart from [analyzing his own] writing, there are two prospects to which Pavese continually recurs. One is the prospect of suicide...The other is the prospect of romantic love and erotic failure. Pavese shows himself as tormented by a profound sense of sexual inadequacy, which he bulwarked by all sorts of theories about sexual technique, the hopelessness of love, and the sex war. Remarks on the predatoriness, the exploitativeness of women are interspersed with confessions of his own failure to love, or to provide sexual satisfaction. Pavese, who never married, records in the journal the reactions to a number of long affairs and casual sex experiences, usually at the point when he is expecting trouble or after they actually have failed. The women themselves are never described; the events of the relationship are not even alluded to."

*

From the diaries of Cesare Pavese—16th October, 1938:

It is not the actual enjoyment of pleasure that we desire. What we want is to test the futility of that pleasure, so as to be no longer obsessed by it.

*

From the diaries of Cesare Pavese—21st December, 1939:

Love is the cheapest of religions.

*

From the diaries of Cesare Pavese—1st June, 1940:
Why do people adopt poses, play the dandy, the skeptic, the stoic or the careless trifler? Because they feel there is something superior in facing life according to a standard and a discipline they have imposed on themselves, if only in their mind. And, in fact, this is the secret of happiness; to adopt a pattern of behavior, a style, a mold into which all our impressions and expressions must fall and be remodeled. Every life lived according to a pattern that is consistent, comprehensive and vital, has a classic symmetry.

*

Leaving aside Pavese's vast chasm of suicidal sadness and regret, not to mention his penchant for deeply negative and often misogynistic thought, it is startling how much insight can be gained from reading the writer's diaries. Setting down his many different selves on the page, Pavese comes to no conclusions. But it's all there in his willingness to examine.

*

Needling himself over and over and over, examine.

*

The unexamined life is not worth living.

*

And yet.

*

In "The artist as exemplary sufferer" Sontag goes on to assert:

> "What Pavese has to say about love is the familiar other side of romantic idealization. Pavese rediscovers, with Stendhal, that love is an essential fiction; it is not that love sometimes makes mistakes, but that it is, essentially, a mistake. What one takes to be an attachment to another person is unmasked as one more dance of the solitary ego…Love, like art, becomes a medium of self-expression."

*

Adopting a specific pose, the pickup artist succeeds admirably. Having succeeded, though, he's forced to reckon with his triumphant self time and time again. His pleasure, then, is ultimately an exercise in futility, obsessively hard-earned. Sisyphus and his boulder rolling away from him, same story and sensation every night.

*

The more sex had, the better one should feel about one's ability as a lover. In my case, though, the opposite proved true. Still shy, still nervous. Blinking too much, I played with my hair. In dull black and white terms, I couldn't stop thinking about everything and nothing, lacking all balance.

No description from any woman is necessary, no events from any of the relationships I had need be recounted or alluded to in detail.

Self at the expense of all else.

*

"I've been losing since I lost my virginity…I feel promiscuous but maybe I'm a prude" Daddy Issues sings on "I'm Not." Years before hearing these lyrics of Jenna Moynihan's, such is the self-constructed box I found myself in.

*

Louise Glück's poem "Mock Orange" begins:

It is not the moon, I tell you.
It is these flowers
lighting the yard.

I hate them.
I hate them as I hate sex,
the man's mouth
sealing my mouth, the man's
paralyzing body—

and the cry that always escapes,
the low, humiliating
premise of union—

*

"Mock Orange" ends with the speaker repudiating the scent of the mock orange, its dreaded constancy, its flowering a burden that the speaker can no longer take, refuses to. "How can I rest? / How can I be content/ when there is still/ that odor in the world?" read the poem's final lines.

*

It's not the sexual act that the speaker of "Mock Orange" hates. (Although there is that.) Nor is it the surrendering of self that sex insists on, the, as Glück's speaker puts it, "question and pursuing answer/ fused in one sound/ that mounts and mounts and then/ is split into the old selves,/ the tired antagonisms." (Although there is that also.)

Instead it's the sexual *expectation* that "Mock Orange's" speaker takes such grave issue with, an expectation that takes desire as a given. Wanting always as knowing and vice-versa when, in fact, the opposite is more often true—the more we want the less we know. The folly of desire is that it will not resist and for Glück's speaker the only respite to this is to not allow a cry to escape in the first place, her mouth sealed. Let the flowers perfume the air with their blooming—she will not be there to smell their scent.

*

After receiving my M.A. in Bellingham, I applied and was accepted into a PhD program at the University of Missouri, causing me to move towns and regions again, this time from Bellingham's Pacific Northwest to Columbia's Midwest. My whole existence prior to the move having been spent on the West Coast, I was now far from all my friends and family. Without fully knowing what I was doing, upon my arrival in Missouri I became celibate—for a year, one single year, which turned into three full years. No sex, no new partners. This celibacy was another loving act of the self, only in a (purely) different way than I'd ever previously experienced.

*

"[T]he man's mouth/ sealing my mouth, the man's/ paralyzing body"— I was sick of being a sealant, no matter how temporary or tenuous.

*

But of course it was much more than that.

*

XVII. A new love puts flight to an old one.

*

"Love is a thing full of anxious fear."

*

Twenty-nine years old.

*

The first year of celibacy was planned. The next two years were not.

*

In his *The Devil's Dictionary*, Ambrose Bierce's definition of prude reads: "A bawd hiding behind the back of her demeanor."

*

For that first year, then, this became the opposite of me: if I'd taken a break from love and sex it wasn't because I'd triumphed over them in any way. It was because they'd, temporarily at least (or so I told my self), triumphed over me. Rather than being righteously declamatory, espousing to anyone within earshot how my-way-was-the-best-way, my willfully celibate demeanor might instead be categorized as insouciantly adrift. I played the knowing fool, too cool for school. I knew the joke, which is why I couldn't bother being in on it.

*

"I shall be chaste and pure,
virgin, intact, untouchable.

I shall touch no being
...
I am by essence clean and pure.
I am pure because I am clean.
I am clean because I am pure"

proclaims Antonin Artaud in his text "I Hate and Renounce as a Coward."

*

"disguised as
a choice of a
body
I say shit
to everything
and
I
go to sleep"

proclaims Antonin Artaud in his text "Seven Poems [Fragments]."

*

I thought I knew the joke. I thought I knew.

*

Filling the gaps with reading, writing and working out, I thus tried to induce sexual and romantic anorexia in myself. Celibate, I thought endlessly about sex, about masculinity and happiness and shyness and loneliness.

*

Following the death of John Gregory Dunne, her husband of thirty-nine years, Joan Didion called it *The Year of Magical Thinking*, thus, at first glance at least, implying that all those previous years were in one way or another unmagical or rote.

*

I am not self-absorbedly implying that my celibacy—a conscious choice initially made by me— was, in any way, shape or form, akin to the death of a spouse that one has been married to for thirty-nine years.

*

And yet.

*

A distinct childhood memory of mine: seventh grade, aged eleven or twelve, in the middle of a fight on the packed school bus as it barreled us all homeward. Across the aisle, JR swinging at me with full force and completely missing, fisting air. In the moment and without thinking about it, slamming my head hard into the window next to me, drawing blood, then swinging back at JR, solidly connecting with his chin. The punch he saw coming, had cushioned himself for, but the look in JR's eyes at the adamancy of my self-destruction when my head hit the window, his utter surprise and shock.

*

It was something I'd no doubt seen in a movie, that self-inflicted preemptive blow before the blow. Silly kid stuff. But looking back on it today, I can't say I wouldn't do the same again. You have to convince your self before you can convince anyone else.

*

Read *The Year of Magical Thinking* in its entirety, though, and it's soon discovered that Didion is still in some sense waiting for her husband to come home, to quietly return from the hospital and go on living with her with nary a blink. Throughout the book Didion feels reluctant to get rid of her dead husband's possessions, to consider herself a widower. Near the end of the book she writes, "I realize as I write this that I do not want to finish this account...The craziness is receding but no clarity is taking its place. I look for resolution and find none."

Didion's magical thinking isn't a product of fatalistic finality but of optimism. If she simply believes it, believes it fully without reason's petty, logical reservations getting in the way, then her husband will live again, be alive with her in their kitchen, their bedroom, everywhere.

*

At angles, my own magical thinking thought process mirrored Didion's. Maintaining a celibate lifestyle, I thought, would bring me back around again to a more unburdened self, one at turns effervescent and unrestrained. Not childlike but adultly poised and taut, possessed by an optimistic assurance that celibacy would activate in me more meaningful insights and understandings than lovelessly sleeping around had. The magic would be in my degree of calibrated self.

*

From the diaries of Cesare Pavese—30th December, 1937:

The tragedy of well-meaning people is the tragedy of a little man gathering all the blue he can find by the light of dawn, and then, at dusk, groping about in his collection afraid of picking up red, which may, in any case, turn out to be yellow. Conscience is nothing more than a flair, trying to recognize a color by the feel of it.

*

"I don't believe that one should devote his life to morbid self-attention. I believe that someone should become a person like other people" imparts Travis Bickle in Martin Scorsese's *Taxi Driver.*

Bickle's belief, though, fails him. Feverishly thinking while lying on his couch or in his bed, staring in a full-length mirror while talking to himself, Bickle's whole existence in *Taxi Driver* is devoted to the morbidity of self-attention. Attempting to become a person like other people he can only be himself.

*

All my life I'd been a writer, primarily a poet, but only now, isolated a-lonely in the Midwest, did I begin to take it seriously, to focus in. As a way of distancing my mind from my body, then, I took to writing surreal, unemotional, sterilely madcap poems, ones proficient in the moment and largely forgettable a week or two later. Many of these took their titles from statements that writers and artists I was reading or thinking about at the time had made; by using their language in my own work I aimed to reach for the peak they'd already attained.

*

Never enough, my own head.

*

"ONGOING TIME STABBED BY A DAGGER."—RENÉ MAGRITTE

A brain secretes thought as a liver secretes bile. Accidents aren't the same thing as mistakes, but your ideas regarding the difference between the two just might be. From close range the French entomologist Jean-Henri Fabre once fired a cannon at a tree full of relentlessly chirping cicadas and not a note of their song was altered, not a beat missed. They were entirely undisturbed. This proves not that cicadas are deaf; it merely proves that cicadas are not thinking while searching—singing—for a mate, and certainly not about cannon blasts. The massed brain secretes each and every thought as the liver secretes vacuous, guileful, greenish-orange bile. Even when absent, out of view, bile itself is a kind of thought; the liver, however, decidedly not. A white semicircle stapled to a piece of black construction paper and taped on the ceiling we painted a watery dull yellow, lots of unattributable wings floating around, I've been working on my idea for a map of the entire universe. In love with its own faultiness, it's a work in progress, plangent thoughts inside plangent thought.

*

"AT THE ORIGIN OF EVERYTHING IS COMMERCE."—DONNA STONECIPHER

We were a pair of lonely sexual markets, each hinging on the social development of our various foreign outputs. Everything for me was a dilemma—imports and exports, the rational anti-rationalization towards the inherency of free will and trade. You had the opposite problem: Incoming and outgoing, your goods had been accepted so easily for so often and so long that they were of little worth to you or anyone else. We came together like two gigantic icebergs mired in a child's empty wading pool. Nothing else to lean against, nothing else to touch. *It's a joy selling quality products again to someone that actually appreciates them* you said with a smile. *My how money has the power to change the world to the point where now I'm finally able to see it* I lovingly replied. So much is paradise, marketwise and fleeting. And the problems that never start never stop. Then behind every window another potential partner or secret admirer, everywhere in sight a more alluring sale or possible trade.

*

Writing such poems, I believed I'd found my calling. Hindsight, however, teaches me that I'd only found another way of enacting my prudery, this time within my celibate self. No matter how much discovery and imagination the poems contained, they were still distancing, a distancing.

*

I love poetry. But it's a complicated, confounding artform. Why can't a thing ever just *be*, without any qualifiers or additions or alterations? In its obfuscating verve and grace, poetry can sometimes seem lazy, even worthless. Loving a thing for what it does not do, cannot do—it is in this way that I have often come to embrace the world.

*

And yet.

*

In his essay "Against Joie de Vivre," Phillip Lopate goes to great length to argue against the simple and happy life, stating, vis-à-vis enjoyment of great sex, "To know rapture is to have one's whole life poisoned." For Lopate the joy of life is, ultimately, boring, bourgeois, almost pedantic. Or, it's not that he finds the good life itself so lackluster, but the way that life corresponds to Lopate's particular schema for accessing the world. In the essay's final paragraph he writes:

> "[*Joie de vivre* is] ...too compensatory. I don't really know what I'm waiting for. I know only that until I have gained what I want from this

> life, my expressions of gratitude and joy will be restricted to variations of a hunter's alertness. I give thanks to a nip in the air that clarifies the scent. But I think it hypocritical to pretend satisfaction while I am still hungry."

*

Nothing Feels Good is the title of rock band The Promise Ring's second album, one called "the quintessential emo record" by music website *Pitchfork*.

*

As a symbolic piece of jewelry, a promise ring, of course, designates the relationship commitment of the ring-bearer to the ring-giver. An engagement ring before the engagement ring, albeit one that shares in a promise of what's to come. In this way a promise ring differs from a purity ring, which symbolizes the wearer's commitment to a chaste lifestyle, sexually beholden to no one. Out in the fleshly, physical world, I've never worn any of these rings on my fingers. Which isn't to say that the sentiment behind them is something foreign or distasteful to me.

*

Consisting of a static-filled melody, limbic piano chasing limbic guitar, "How Nothing Feels," the sixth track on *Nothing Feels Good*, is instrumental only, sans lyrics. Slightly more upbeat than "How Nothing Feels" but still defiantly emotional, the lyrics to the title track to the album read, in part:

I don't know God
And I don't know anyone
And I don't know God
And I don't know if anything at all will be all right
I've got my hands on the one end
And I don't know where to put them

*

Celibate that first year, I understood Lopate's hunger for what might not ever materialize, understood The Promise Ring's invocation that "I've got my hands on the one end/ And I don't know where to put them." Whether it's the joy of life, the joy of sex, or simply where to put one's arms at the end of a good concert where they've been less limbs than conduits unto fraught and freeing sound, renunciation of anything is arduous work, especially if it involves something you were conflicted about in the first place.

*

Discovering, though, that the race runs even when you're not in it—and you don't mind that fact—is, initially, revelatory; there are so many other ways to engage the world. I studied books like Lewis Hyde's *The Gift: Creativity and Art in the Modern World* and Christopher Lane's *Shyness: How Normal Behavior Became a Sickness*, read dusty and shiny poetry collections by French surrealists and Russian absurdists, wrote more of my own poems. Listening rather than waiting to talk, I heard what I'd previously ignored or simply cast off as inconsequential. To everywhere and nowhere, my dog and I walked. A lapsed Catholic, occasionally I even went to church to smell the incense, admire the gilded pageantry. With some success I tried to, wherever I went that year, not carry around my self, the sexual one, the endlessly absorbed and involved one.

*

Soon after it was published, 1583 comments were posted online regarding Stephen Marche's *New York Times* Nov 25 2017 op-ed "The Unexamined Brutality of the Male Libido," which begins with the sentence: "After weeks of continuously unfolding abuse scandals, men have become, quite literally, unbelievable."

Recommended by 694 readers and chosen as one of the newspaper-approved *NYT Picks* comments, HL from AZ writes: "I have a cat and feed it. It wants to kill every single day. I buy fish at the store and want to fish. I buy meat and want to hunt. I kept my promise to my wife of fidelity while still desiring other women. I aspire to be a gentleman and be part of a civil society. We live on a food chain that's violent and brutal. We also have self control and self awareness.

"We must do much better our survival depends on it."

Not a *NYT Picks* comment and recommended by just se
Wheels from Portland, Oregon writes: "Thank you for this
what has been needed to be addressed, men's dirty little se
sex at all cost. If they talk about their fixation, they might have to do
about it, like deny themselves."

*

After stating the existence of male unbelievability in its opening, Marche's "The Unexamined Brutality of the Male Libido" goes on to examine and castigate the silence woven into contemporary masculinity and its attendant dickly urges. Marche asserts that, "The masculine libido and its accompanying forces and pathologies drive so much of culture and politics and the economy, while remaining more or less unexamined, both in intellectual circles and in private life" and how, post sex-ed class in high school, "Men deal with their nature alone, and apart. Ignorance and misprision are the norms." The piece ends declaratively, with Marche writing, "If you want to be a civilized man, you have to consider what you are. Pretending to be something else, some fiction you would prefer to be, cannot help. It is not morality but culture—accepting our monstrosity, reckoning with it—that can save us. If anything can."

*

My own celibacy occurred years before the MeToo'd Harvey Weinstein-Charlie Rose-Roger Ailes-centric "weeks of continuously unfolding abuse scandals" but many of the points Marche makes in the piece—as well as ones made by the commentators—ring true with me. Personally, my sexual history was a case study in contradiction: shy and deferential around women, ever resistant to making the first move but nevertheless selfish in my pursuit; insularly insecure but outwardly self-assured, even cocky. Desirous of love, I masked such a desire beneath jokes and half-truths, all of them serving to hopefully assuage my own sense of stereotypical masculine deficiency. Being both prudish and a cad of a certain kind, it sounds like a joke—but, sleeping around, attempting to sleep around, I believed in my self with a resilient fervor. If Marche overstates certain things in "The Unexamined Brutality of the Male Libido" he does so knowing that at least some of his contentions aren't, out loud or in print, stated often enough.

.the rotten masks that divide one man/ from another, one man from himself… the desolation/ of being man, and all its glories" writes Octavio Paz in his poem "Sunstone."

*

"I let my memories fall through/ It's not my fault/ I blame my sexuality" Daddy Issues sings on "I'm Not."

*

"I let my memories fall through/ It's not my fault/ I blame my sexuality" Daddy Issues sings on "I'm Not."

*

"I've got my hands on the one end/ And I don't know where to put them" The Promise Ring sings on "How Nothing Feels."

*

A Year of Magical Thinking. Twenty-nine years old.

*

Celibate that first year in the Midwest I felt relief from my libido and inherent male gaze launched outward. Leaking its covert imagination everywhere, especially on women, I felt relief from the (sexual) daimon constantly prowling along and inside me.

This isn't to say, though, that I felt any more civilized or cultured. Rather, I somehow felt inappropriately intimate with my self, a thing I didn't previously know was possible. No matter the reason, to be a chastely adult in a thoroughly sexualized world is to be a specific type of *other*, grasping for the austereness of a personal vision that the vast majority of people can't fathom, let alone see.

*

Having first started abstaining in 1985 when she was 37 and her marriage was ending, seminal conceptual artist Adrian Piper's celibacy helped her "to transcend the drag of the body," giving her the restorative energy that partnered sex had so often depleted her of.

O if only, if only.

*

Inappropriately intimate as in thinking about masturbation with the same regularity as when I'd been uncelibate, but now fixated on the peculiar schisms of the masturbatory, momentary relief compounded by the innate aloneness. ("Masturbation will always be my favorite/ form of sex, although if I was a tree/ I'd just stand there in the breeze" writes Eileen Myles in their poem "Lorna & Vicki" but the longer one waits— gestural, frantic, immobile— the more they might soon shiver.) Inappropriately intimate as in constantly questioning the contours and constricts of the box I'd chosen to live within, an entombing creviced at every corner by illumination. But what's to see when, standing in the darkness, all is blinding light?

*

"Instead of leaving the box, I shall enclose the world within it" imparts Kobo Abe's box man. When I was younger I didn't know understand what that meant, didn't know how one's box could be less a constriction than a vessel for any number of successful ways of being and believing. At the time I simply assumed that nobody understood who or what was inside. As a result of this surmising, I turned into my self. Perfect risk, I lived like that.

*

Although his parents themselves were not religious, as a child Albert Einstein was devoutly so, attending a Catholic elementary school and clinging hard to the concept of faith. Einstein's religiosity, though, ended abruptly, at the age of twelve. He later wrote, "It is quite clear to me that the religious paradise of youth, which was thus lost, was a first attempt to free myself from the chains of the 'merely personal,' from an existence dominated by wishes, hopes, and primitive feelings." Denouncing religion, the scientist later remarked, had allowed him the freedom to slave himself to science, body and soul. "[B]eing in flight from the I and the we to the it" is how Einstein put it.

*

That flight from primitivity, from the 'merely personal'—Einstein made it his life's work and his many scientific revelations can be the judge of his success or failure. But even Einstein, Mortal among mortals, ended up fallible within his science-as-life enslavement. Both of his marriages were infidelity-filled debacles—discussing his relationship with his first wife, Mileva, in a letter to his eventual second wife (and own cousin) Elsa, he wrote, "I treat my wife as an employee whom I cannot fire. I have my own bedroom and avoid being alone with her"—and when Einstein's schizophrenic second son Eduard died in 1965 his father had not seen him in thirty years.

$E=mc^{2.}$

*

In death or in life, I, we or it, no one knows the circumstances of either the flight's takeoff or arrival. "Vanity of vanities, all is vanity" was one of Einstein's favorite maxims, said with hearty cheer. Of self or science, vanity. Vanity, making a religion of sex, celibacy or love.

*

Entails swaddling one's self in endless theories about the self, all of which are fruitful without ever reaching the roots of the tree actually bearing said fruit, one of my own definitions of prudery.

*

"There's never any center to it. No path, no line. There are great spaces where you pretend there used to be someone, but it's not true, there was no one" writes Marguerite Duras in *The Lover*. And to try and be that someone you once were is to follow a center line that, at hard right and left angles, keeps zigging and zagging.

*

I'm selfish in other words, but only in relation to what I don't know about my self, what I might not, in the end, want to know. And will not stop searching for as a result.

*

From *The Unquiet Grave* Cyril Connolly on equanimity in the face of desire: "Yet no one can achieve Serenity until the glare of passion is past the meridian. There is no certain way of preserving chastity against the will of the body."

*

Constantly greedy for some type of satiation always in the distance, while celibate that year I was. Willpower had cured physically what unknowing desire, though, couldn't contain. The calmness of a center eluded me the more I chased after it.

*

X. Love is always a stranger in the home of avarice.

*

And yet.

*

In the essay collection that contains his "Against Joie de Vivre," that piece of Phillip Lopate's is followed by one entitled "Art of the Creep." In it, Lopate pontificates on what makes people, specifically men, creeps, assholes, good-for-nothing losers, etc. "To me, a creep is someone who walks around as if with a load in his pants... The creep would like to forget that he has a body, which only draws your attention all the more to his ungainly posture..."

*

Chastity is a pose (a mask) like any other and the taller one stands within it the more attention is often drawn to them. To dissect the various 21st century manifestations of creepery is futile, and surely not all of them entail walking around as if with a load deposited in one's pants. Experience attests that there are different shades and textures, each affected by age and living location, social attitudes, proclivities and demeanors, and on and on. In my own purview, conscious, willful celibacy at the age of twenty-nine while physically fit and reasonably intelligent, attractive and composed turns one into a minorly creepy assemblage of disparate parts, especially if one is living in Columbia, Missouri . On learning the news, the inquisitiveness I received from others, regardless of sex, gender or age, no matter if I was at the bar or gym, coffee shop or university library, was deferential and often (Midwestern Nice!) respectful. Within the confines of that respect, though, lurked overtones of my weirdness, my untrammeled oddity, half-creepy in its self-aware thwartedness.

*

As one of my close friends at the time, T, put it, *You're kind of acting like a freak, dude, with this.*

*

Although no doubt partially true, T's attitude, a common one, belies what subsequent research has made clear to me is a more regular occurrence than might otherwise be realized. My own brand of (willful) secular celibacy was internalized and solitary; single, not in a relationship, I made a conscious choice not to have sex of any kind with anyone for a full calendar year. But, in passing, discussing what I was working on while emailing with W (a now semi-distant friend who I once lived with for a year during my early twenties) he mentions that between the ages of twenty-two and twenty-seven, for five whole years, he was in a sexless relationship with his girlfriend at the time, a woman who he was in love with and who he thought would become his wife. (It was on her initiative that they eventually broke up.) When asked about the specifics of their relationship dynamic, W writes:

Maybe it sounds pathetic, especially now, years later, but I'm not totally sure why. Early on we reached an unspoken impasse and then…it just continued. I knew that she'd been a born-again virgin before, had declared that to people. But that term never came up when we were dating. We just didn't have sex and I did with myself what I did on the side. I wouldn't exactly say I was celibate. Or that we were celibate. We didn't have sex but I loved her and I did at the time question a lot. But I didn't bring it up with her directly, not even at the end.

Another friend in a similar relationship for a much shorter interval, just nine months, writes, *There are obviously a lot of ways to express love and affection without sex. There are way more of those than just plain sex, however you're even defining sex here.*

*

Obviously, yes. But beyond the clichés of the sexless marriage, product of some twenty-five or thirty-year partnership that was once filled with passionate ardor and now, so many years later, is simply a medley of familiarity and brittleness, the secular celibate relationship is rarely discussed or commented on. This might be due to its relative rarity; perhaps I've weirder friends than most. Or it might be due to the lack of rote segmentation that something like celibate-while-in-a-committed-and-caring-relationship-while-also-young-and-disease-free-and-unreligious-and-virile-and-capable-and-all-systems-go-*ready* slots into. Category-less, its category is its own.

*

It is not the actual enjoyment of pleasure that we desire. What we want is to test the futility of that pleasure, so as to be no longer obsessed by it states Cesare Pavese in his diaries. Constantly rammed up against the futility of one's pleasure, ever-obsessively desirous. Whole lives are lived like that.

*

"Song Against Sex," the first track on cult indie rock heroes Neutral Milk Hotel's first album *On Avery Island*, passes, in three verses, through a kaleidoscope of imagery, alliteration and metaphor, some of it deeply concrete, some of it disjunctive to the point of abstraction. At the beginning of the song's third verse Jeff Mangum, Neutral Milk Hotel's bandleader, famed for his lyrical childlike innocence, sings of attacking pleasure points and pictures ripped out from pornographic magazines. Before the song ends elsewhere, possibly hinting at suicide, Mangum declaims the societal lie that sex can be at certain times for certain people, a lie that hurts far more than it balms or gratifies. Asked in an interview after *On Avery Island*'s release if sex "grossed him out," Magnum replied:

I'm grossed out about sex being used as a tool for power, about people not giving a shit about who they're putting their dick into. I find that to be really upsetting. I've known a lot of people that have been heavily damaged by some asshole's drunken hard-on. And that stuff really upsets me. It's not against sex itself. All those sexual references are like...

About specific personal references?

Yeah.

*

Not against sex itself but against the personal references one has to, like it or not, ponder when thinking or acting sexually. Sex as a tool for power, to be sure, but also as something that loses imaginative luster the better one gets at it.

*

Orientation doesn't seem to matter with regards to any of this hesitation or questioning either. Taken from his collection *Proxies: Essays Near Knowing*, Brian Blanchfield's essay "On Frottage" asserts: "It was at first a surprise to me at twenty-two, and then a kind of—like sex itself: repeatable, singular—discovery I came to expect, that the partners I found (finding me) in New York were, same as in [Blanchfield's home state of] North Carolina, rarely expressly into penetration… All four *longer* relationships I had in my ten years in New York excluded anal sex altogether."

In the relationships that Blanchfield is discussing in "On Frottage" satisfaction is claimed— "Frottage is a rather broad category of consensual, nonpenetrative, (usually) hands-free sex…" reads the author's definition early in the essay—and the bulk of the piece is in fact devoted to the stark perils of being young, gay and full-throatedly alive in the unknown during the 1980s and 1990s. "I never had a sex life without having a status. The two were inextricable. My early fantasy of partnership was in fact sealed fast by HIV…"

For Blanchfield to be sexually non-penetrative when he was younger was a specific kind of choice based, in part, around safety. Frottage is not celibacy, perhaps, but, in keeping with the nearness of *Proxies'* title, near celibacy. A kind of prudent hesitation (wisely prudish?) that still contains its own exclamation, impossible to misinterpret.

*

Further, that sex isn't comprised of one single thing but instead a thousand and eleven wildly different things isn't something I much considered at the time. My vision of sexuality and its attendant worlds was laughably narrow and static back then. I hadn't read or engaged with any queer theory or theorists; didn't understand that the standard happiness scripts that I thought I saw everywhere around me were, in fact, oftentimes vast sources of alienation and oppression for both those invested in their illusion and the wider world at large. Heteronormative to the core, unthinkingly so, I simply took my sexual desires to be everyone else's. When you're young, you're young—it's not an excuse so much as a lamentation. Even sadder, I wasn't that young.

*

You're kind of acting like a freak, dude, with this. But in various shades we're all out here or were out here or will be, some of us contemplative, others ill-content, all of us closely examining our selves in one way or another. Each of us, of course, terminally unique.

Looking back, what I realize now is that my personal intimacy wasn't inappropriate exactly. It was simply attempting to adhere to a self that, moment to moment, I could not place. Sexual and desirous but choosing to not have sex; outwardly social, even gregarious (soon after my arrival in Columbia, I began co-hosting a local literary reading series and, five miles from campus, my small ivy-walled house also became the go-to Friday night afterhours destination for some of my fellow student-friends and me) but yet deeply lonely; introverted by nature but easily extroverted on cue (at the time of my chastity I was teaching writing to undergraduates at MU, the biggest public university in the state, with each of my classes containing 25+ students).

*

As that first year of celibacy progressed to its end, though, I was happy in many ways! Magical thinking and (not) doing had made me a better communicator and a more diligent, earnest listener and confidante. If to a degree I was still shy and selfish I'd also worked on negotiating and owning both those aspects of my self, more cognizant and willing to give myself a break for them. *Acceptance Now-Serenity Later* became my *Seinfeld*-inspired unofficial mantra. Saying it under my breath while jogging or in the gym was a total joke, sure. And true nevertheless.

Still, without knowing what the specific underlying ailment is asceticism cures nothing, and to be anorexic (in my case sexually and romantically) is an attempt to misrecognize symptom for cause. But the power of a different perspective *does* have power and for me that willfully celibate year was a positive one. Masculine solidifier, my (shy, sly) mouth all those previous years constantly sealing or trying to seal itself atop a woman's, my imagination's positive qualities, its negative qualities, its relentlessness in terms of sex, daimonic, some perfect necessity or so I thought— that year of celibacy tempered my self's semblance to a different timbre than I previously knew existed. Resisting, and in doing so became a particular variety of free.

*

And yet.

*

At her ninetieth birthday party my grandmother, walking into the restaurant, took my arm and said, "You get old and you have to recharge but if you're lucky you don't *feel* any different, you just don't."

*

I turned thirty, newly self-declared uncelibate. I felt younger than I had in a long while.

*

Googling the phrase "30 is the new 20" elicits, as of this writing, 12,060,000,000 hits. Some of those results argue against the phrase's mentality, others for it. Regardless of any particular take, though, "30 is the new 20" is a universally ubiquitous saying and has been for some time.

*

One of my own definitions of prudery entails, having ridden before, fully understanding how to do so again, fully apprehending how pedaling connects with speed and where, on first approach, to put one's body. To start, stop, slow down, the pressures and fluences that must be constantly calibrated. Knowing well all those things but, in an instant, forgetting them, falling down or not even being able to sit atop properly, let alone start moving. The easier it is the harder it can be.

*

It's like riding a—

*

I myself cringe at that 30/20 phrase. Nor do I think that by denying the credence of a thing—in this case an age—can it be transmogrified into a state of existing that is, drop of a hat, more carefree or youthful.

*

Nevertheless when, four months into my uncelibate self-declaration, after my slow and instant realization that dating and trying to date in the Midwest is very different as compared to dating in the West, especially when, without truly realizing it, one has turned from a young into an OLD, that years-long process made, odd gray hair turned into a burgeoning clump of odd gray hairs, overnight, she approached me in the bar I, knowing little, knew what to do.

*

In his *Shrinking Violets: The Secret Life of Shyness* (2017) cultural critic and shy person Joe Moran writes that Americans "have a reputation for seeing shyness as un-American." Moran cites Teddy Roosevelt's speech "The Strenuous Life" as an example of Unabashed American Want that, then and now, has no time for reticent downward glances and surreptitious half-smiles.

*

Given in Chicago on April 10, 1899, Roosevelt's speech begins:

> *I wish to preach, not the doctrine of ignoble ease, but the doctrine of the strenuous life, the life of toil and effort, of labor and strife; to preach that highest form of success which comes, not to the man who desires mere easy peace, but to the man who does not shrink from danger, from hardship, or*

from bitter toil, and who out of these wins the splendid ultimate triumph.

Un-American Shyness, then, is acceptance of ignoble ease. The willingness to pine, to imagine, but not actually get. A repudiation of the splendid ultimate triumph, shyness is a giving in without putting up a fight.

*

On the other hand, in its egotistical self-absorption, its subconscious insistence that my *I* is preciously different than everyone else's *I* around me, shyness seems to be inherently American. Actively not looking at you, praying to not arouse your attention, you soon look at me with curiosity.

*

And yet.

*

In the bar she approached and, recognizing her, I guessed her name wrong, once, twice, thrice. *Wait, are you sure you know it?* She smirked at that, nodded. *Begins with a V?* I rapid-fired. *A Q? Z?* Eyes wide, she smiled broadly. *Heavens to Jesus!* she said, her voice deep and seemingly astonished. *That's beyond amazing! Because my first name actually starts with a Q, my middle with a V and my last name is Zardar.* She waited for my reaction before smiling again, this time in a far less affected way. *Do you do tarot too? Or read palms?* She was, clearly, fucking with me.

No, her name was M and now that we had an understanding we could talk without concern for meddlesome matters like social propriety and decorum. Could, heavens to Jesus, just pretend we knew one and other well already and in pretending a reality would soon surface. Born and raised in Missouri, M was twenty-six, a visual artist moonlighting as a flight attendant. It was also soon discovered that neither of us knew the last name of the mutual friend we had in common. I liked her immediately and I liked her more five minutes after that.

Walking home from Doc's later there was the stir of neon inside me, something *new.* Our flirty favorite-comedians-and horror-story-comedy-club-performance-talk at the bar, the circumstances of her writing her phone number on my wallet (long story). Her early back door exit, my eyes trailing her body as she walked, the idiosyncratic red skirt and red fanny pack (when you're young, you're young) combo she wore, her shoulder length strawberry blonde hair—it's all still there as I watch from afar.

*

What's important for me to recall now, though, is that when, towards the end of that first night at Doc's, M said she wanted to come home and watch a DVD with me I demurred, instead asking her if she wanted to go on a walk in the park the next day. When, a date later, she did eventually come back to my place, she left an hour after her arrival; we'd shared a semi-sterile series of kisses and nothing more. Postponed once, our third date was also our final one and, taking place at an empty bar, can only be described as anticipation-free enjoyable. The relationship hadn't been anything to begin with but, a half-hour in, the nothing that was was clearly over.

*

XV. Every lover regularly turns pale in the presence of his beloved.

*

I'd liked M and she'd liked me. We'd desired one and other on equal terms. The difference between our approach to that desire, though, proved to be everything. In my timidity and unwillingness to be overt, M understandably assumed I wasn't that interested in her. And with each subsequent date and Richard-Pryor-is-God conversation the more attracted to M I became the less I outwardly showed it.

*

From the diaries of Cesare Pavese—31st October, 1940:

Here is the proof that you are wholly made of pride: now that she has given you permission... you not only do not do so, but you do not even feel any burning desire to...If we know we can do a thing, we are satisfied, and perhaps do not do it at all.

*

Why? Heavens to Jesus why?

*

"...If you are truly in love and your lover says things which make you happy, you will lose the power of speech" is Stendhal's declaration in *On Love*. Far from being a marker of deficient fervor, "shyness is a proof of love" according to Stendhal and for a true acolyte less is always more, incremental displays of affection and attention being far more significant than, say, making clear to your object of desire that you like her by sleeping with her on the third date, or straightforwardly letting her know at the end of the second date that you like spending time with her, want to see her again soon, tomorrow, more right now.

Writing in the early 19th century, Stendhal's conception-of-love lineage could yet be tied to Andreas Capellanus's chivalric tradition as captured in his 12th century treatise *The Art of Courtly Love*. Which is to say that both authors are, circa the 21st century, hopelessly out of date. "Modern love is meant to be the coming together of enlightened self-interest, with partners offering intimacy and commitment in return for the same...In an age that values emotional mutuality, unrequited love signals immaturity and low self-esteem" states Joe Moran in *Shrinking Violets: The Secret Life of Shyness.*

Surely Moran is right here, his logic and reasoning sound. Even if compared to previous generations Millennials sleep with fewer people and do so later in life, this is still the age of Tinder, Bumble and Chaturbate, of friends-with-benefits and pickup artists. Exclusively gaining one's perspective on love from (male) authors like Stendhal and Capellanus leaves the contemporary love-seeker stranded in the past, panning for gold in some long-forgotten mountain stream while everyone else mines crypto in a humming din of advanced awareness.

Still, one point directly made by Stendhal (and indirectly by Capellanus) cannot be discounted, it being the balancing act that love (true and eternal) calls for; how its whole artistry "seems to... consist in saying precisely what the degree of intoxication requires at any given moment" and learning those degrees and their various intoxicatory properties can be an infinitely complicated process. Imagination is required, as is a fine-tuned sense of calibration. Promises are pointless, mere language particles, and failure or success can be difficult to gauge or predict. What's dysfunctional or disjointed for one set of lovers is foundation of understanding and attraction for another set.

*

In the actual moment, amorous, a lilting soft look from her or something less visible but more perceived, unmistakably foretold beginnings of a soon to be foregone conclusion, what fills my head is a distinct type of pressure that also imbues my limbs. So badly do I want, which is why I might initially fight against. Attempting to find the secret to always loving for the first time and instead suddenly feeling tethered in my head to a tepid *sameness* that's, paradoxically, completely foreign to me each and every time I encounter it. Thus I hang back, I overthink, I question my motives and her signals and what is actually happening between two people sitting on one couch or lying on one bed. Stampeding the moment with indecision, I doubt. Denial is a door that I continually open and close behind me. I have the only key but I keep changing the lock anyway.

*

In his famous 1841 essay "Self-Reliance" Emerson writes:

"To believe your own thought, to believe that what is true for you in your private heart is true for all men, — that is genius. Speak your latent conviction, and it shall be the universal sense; for the inmost in due time becomes the outmost."

For long years I've wondered about these contentions of Emerson's, have come to no real conclusion. Certainly I've never felt like a genius but then again universal sense, even our conception of self-reliance, is very different now as compared to when Emerson was alive and writing. What is true in my private heart seems to only and forever be mine, but I wonder if therein lies my entire scope of vanity.

Terminally unique.

*

Once you learn how to ride the bike you never forget. But what if you did, if you couldn't help but forget? If, for whatever (heavens to Jesus) reason, you even wanted to forget?

*

The history of prudery is a history of the fear of the unknown, alluring pleasurescapes filled, past their candy-shell exterior, with potential shame, awkwardness and discomfort. Even if it's of the lusty variety, a veneer of anticipatory ill-ease pervading through every cell and pore. Especially with someone I don't know that well, *not* putting a protruding part of my body into their body—as good as doing so can feel, which it does feel, it does feel very good—can seem *natural* to me, not the other way around. In love, limerent, within the passionate confines of desire imaginative and unrestrained, all's a different story, although even then at times I've experienced momentary reservation. But so much of my life has been filled with physical and emotional departures and arrivals, half-steps turned full and then, looking blindly back into the sun, pivoted back around again.

*

Later, thinking Freudianly despite my aversion to his way of thought, I told my *well-it's-for-the-best* self that M looked too much like my mother. That she was too young, that the fact that she was recently out of a two year-long relationship and I out of a year-long period of celibacy had, for both of us, activated an unhealthy sense of expectation. How, in keeping with that theme, everything about our unrelationship had been preordained in some sense. If it had reached that point, surely the end would have been found in the beginning. Ravenously fucking soon after meeting, then casually dating for a few months before growing bored with one and another and drifting apart, unrelationship not even worth an actual breakup. Text me later—or not.

So can extend my malignant imaginative scope when romance or its possibility is involved. The sky is not blue, the grass is not green. Resigned to their fate, the waves don't crash into the shore so much as wilt into the sand, already dead.

*

"A kind of twin that prowls alongside, most often vivid when things are tough, pushing you toward the life you signed up to live before you fell into the amnesia of birth and forgot the whole affair, my daimon, my imagination" imparts Mary Ruefle.

How tough can it be?
Still tougher.

*

Or, mixing self-criticality with healthy splashes of remorse and shame, such was my unproductive way of dealing with rejection at the time. However frothily full, all glasses are half-empty.

*

"Snatching defeat from the jaws of victory" is how heroin-addicted hero guitarist Johnny Thunders's entire existence is described in Legs McNeil and Gillian McCain's book *Please Kill Me: The Uncensored Oral History of Punk.* Every time he or his band got a break Thunders would somehow ruin it. The music he was able to create, though, kept people—managers, promoters, fans, bandmates, lovers—coming back. It lasts even if he and his failures do not.

*

Love and the desire for it is madness, a "disease of the soul" declares Stendhal ad nauseum in *On Love.* It's not an original thought, no. But two or two hundred years later it is one easy to return to again and again.

*

"The self is a set of linguistic patterns" imparts author Helen DeWitt in a 2016 *New York* magazine feature largely focused on her frustration with the publishing industry not fully understanding her or her work. DeWitt is a speaker of, not including English, fourteen different languages: Latin, ancient Greek, French, German, Spanish, Italian, Portuguese, Dutch, Danish, Norwegian, Swedish, Arabic, Hebrew, and Japanese. "Reading and speaking in another language is like stepping into an alternate history of yourself where all the bad connotations are gone" is how DeWitt has dealt with her personal and artistic distresses. By reducing her self to language, DeWitt has enacted a fully comprehensive sense of it. She walks in Latin, she scratches her arm in Dutch and flushes the toilet in ancient Greek. All the bad connotations are thus erased by DeWitt's ability to distend, through language, who she is into who she'd like to be. If she can't fix the broken toaster in French perhaps she can do so in German.

*

A distinct childhood memory of mine: learning Spanish with L in 7th grade, L being the first girl I ever kissed, really truly kissed.

(In 6th grade I'd pecked J outside the bathrooms just after 2:00 recess but that'd hardly been a kiss, and after its occurrence we barely spoke to one and other again. Prior to our lips briefly touching, I'd asked J, "Can you kiss someone while wearing a hat?" Being surprised by the question and not knowing what to say, she responded, "I don't think so. But I don't wear hats. And I've never kissed anyone." I took my hat off and forty-five seconds after my nervous approach J and I went our separate ways.)

All year long we were group partners, L and I, and we stumbled into the language together, her *Yo no se* my *Yo también*. But we were both diligent, earnest learners. Being that my mom was a 3rd grade teacher at an ESOL elementary school and L's stepdad was Mexican American, originally born outside Juárez, both of us wanted to finagle some hold on the language, however precarious. On Sundays I'd go to L's house on the other side of town to study the past and future tenses and while doing so we'd make out in her always-absent older brother's bedroom. Cooler than me, L introduced me to Pink Floyd and Jefferson Airplane. She was a snowboarder, a good one, and had the goggle tan to prove it. She cleaned out her pet snake Fidel's cage not because she was told to by her parents, but because it was needed, because that's what you did when you had a pet snake. When L and I kissed she bit my tongue, sometimes lightly, sometimes hard. When I asked my friends about it they told me that wasn't normal, not at all. *No me importó. No lo cuestioné.* I bit back.

*

Entails longing's ache being, in its purity, magnified to a greater degree than the self's myriad linguistic patterns might truly warrant, a trading of bad connotations for worse denotations, one of my own definitions of prudery.

*

And yet.

*

A decade and a half later, I translated a few poems by the Mexican poet Octavio Paz, ones specifically written during Paz's early career infatuation with French Surrealism. Entitled "Here," the best of them reads:

My footsteps in the street
resonate

in another street
where

I hear my footsteps
crossing into the street
where

the only thing true is the mist in the fog

L might have been interested to read it, but we'd lost touch immediately after middle school, with her going to a different high school than me and our adolescent *let's-definitely-stay-in-touch* relationship ending weeks after our final makeout-study session.

To this day I still, on occasion, dream about L. Resonating footsteps, mist true in the fog.

*

After M and the slow, immediate washout, I retreated inside my box once again, this time involuntarily. Feeling lost as to how to *be,* especially romantically, sexually, I turned inward. While willfully celibate I'd been open about my choice and the motivation behind it with anyone who'd been remotely curious. Now, however, I slinked to the corner and peered to the center in silence. Exteriorly I still maintained an amiably distant façade—cool guy but now less than triumphantly so, a bit worried to still be at the bar at last call again—but interiorly I shelled my feelings piecemeal, bit by self-reflective bit. Having gone on only a handful of dates in Missouri while uncelibate, none being noteworthy, I stopped online dating and I stopped looking to date while out in the wider world. Always at the same bars as last week, on Friday, the only day I went out, I regularly drank with friends downtown, but the extent of my sociality on that night was alcohol-related and immediate to people I already knew, none of whom were romantic options. Still in school but now no longer taking actual classes, solely working on my dissertation, I continued teaching at MU but left immediately after doing so each day, rarely mingling with my colleagues. The reading series I had been co-hosting each month turned irregular and the leaves on the oak tree that citadelled my house fell to the ground, changing colors as they did so, dying, dead. Letting each drift away of its own accord, wind's scattered whims, I didn't rake or pile them up. I lived alone with my dog, with guests rarely coming over to visit.

*

In *Shutting Out the Sun: How Japan Created Its Own Lost Generation* (2006), Michael Zielenziger writes at length on the plight and circumstance of Japanese *hikikomori*, "young men who lock themselves in their rooms and find little solace in the larger society." As Zielenziger relates in *Shutting Out the Sun*, such *hikikomori*—ranging in age from fifteen to thirty-nine, the vast majority of them from the middle-class—tune out fully, shutting themselves in to lives of complete social isolation while yet relying on their parents for food, shelter and overall support. *Hikikomori* seclude themselves out of fear of not being able to match up to either their parents or larger society's vision for them and having done so they enact a self-fulfilling prophecy of their own creation. Numbers vary, but circa 2020 there might be as many as a million and a half *hikikomori* living in Japan—in a country of 128 million citizens, a small number, to be sure, but still a significant one—and the lives they lead are insular and claustrophobic.

Outwardly at least, *hikikomori* also evince little interest in sex. Due to several different factors, including living conditions, societal fixations and family dynamics, Japan as a whole is considered to be one of the least sex-interested countries in the world, with a 2010 national fertility survey revealing that 28% of men and 23% of women between the ages of 18-34 were not involved in romantic and/or sexual relationships with anyone, nor did they want to be involved, and that 28% of single men and 26% of single women between the ages of 35-39 had no sexual experience whatsoever. (Additionally, another 2010 national survey in Japan revealed how 40% of marriages in Japan could be referred to as sexless, at least when that term can be defined as "engaging in sex less than once a month, despite not suffering from any health-related conditions.") Conducted in 2015, a follow up fertility survey in Japan made clear that the 2010 numbers were not misguided or filled with aberrations—if anything, the sexlessness and lack of interest in sex was increasing.

More important than sex for *hikikomori*, however, is the self. Fearing the worst, they do not allow themselves the opportunity to try for the best. They burrow down, box themselves in. Talking to Zielenziger, one former *hikikomori* tells him that "the challenge is to preserve your inner feelings and unique identity while still finding a way to function in the larger world of the collective." This, then, can be exceedingly difficult, especially when that larger collective never seems to slow down or stand still.

*

Isolates of a very different order, the concept of the Western "incel" is one that, although ostensibly simply a person desiring sex and/or a romantic relationship (the term was coined by a queer Canadian woman in the late 1990s) and not being able to find it, has since metastasized into a shorthand term for virulent (and occasionally violent) misogynists of utterly depraved mindsets. Quoting from vitriolic posts ("Women are the ultimate cause of our suffering…We need to focus more on our hatred of women. Hatred is power") made on websites like Reddit and Incels.me, Jia Tolentino writes in her 2018 "The Rage of the Incels" piece on *The New Yorker* website that at the end of the day: "Incels aren't really looking for sex; they're looking for absolute male supremacy. Sex, defined to them as dominion over female bodies, is just their preferred sort of proof." Elsewhere, in an article in *The Guardian* centered on former "incel spokesman" Jack Peterson's subsequent repudiation of the "incel movement" following multiple incidents of violence by the group, the point is made by Peterson that his immersion as an 11-year old in "reject culture," most notably on the website 4chan, influenced his entire sense of victimhood as he grew up. "A lot of incels think they're owed shit from the world. The mindset is kind of like this: 'I've been bullied and rejected my whole life so because of all the suffering I've experienced. Now the world owes me sex, it owes me friends, it owes me success, because of all the failures I've had.'"

Still other think-pieces on incels (nearly all of whom, like *hikikomori*, are from the middle-class) debate their literary origins—"The incel isn't just a monstrous birth of our casually cruel and anonymous internet culture. He is also a product of a literary culture that treats the topic of male sexual frustration as if it is of prime importance to us all" asserts Erin Spampinato in her *Electric Lit* essay "The Literary Roots of the Incel Movement"—and, via conservative columnist Ross Douthat's *New York Times* op-ed "The Redistribution of Sex," the question of incel legitimacy. "If we are concerned about the just distribution of property and money, why do we assume that the desire for some sort of sexual redistribution is inherently ridiculous?" asks Douthat, building off economist Robin Hanson's similar inquiry. Somewhat surprisingly, that question is treated seriously by Douthat, with the breaking down of, in his eyes, the sex vs. power dynamics that are most important circa the present historical moment. Douthat writes how, in his opinion at least:

> "...the dominant message [in Western culture] about sex is still essentially Hefnerian, despite certain revisions attempted by feminists since the heyday of the Playboy philosophy—a message that frequency and variety in sexual experience is as close to a summum bonum as the human condition has to offer, that the greatest possible diversity in sexual desires and tastes and identities should be not only accepted but cultivated, and that virginity and celibacy are at best strange and at worst pitiable states..."

Lamenting how "older ideas about the virtues of monogamy and chastity and permanence and the special respect owed to the celibate" are at this point rusty and antiquated, of a bygone era, Douthat predicts that our future Western world *will,* via virtual reality porn, sex robots or some other technological advance, take "right to sex" arguments and initiatives into account, the same way they once (not entirely successfully) did for labor equality, equal work for equal pay, and property rights.

*

On the face of it *hikikomori* and incels might seem wholly estranged from one and other in type and tone. The former boxes themselves in out of societal desperation, an inability to succeed and conform culturally, whereas the latter lashes out at women specifically over issues that, although ostensibly sexual in nature, are more directly related to notions of control, power and supremacy.

Both groups, however, can be violent. In *Shutting out the Sun* Michael Zielenziger writes that "Although there are no accurate data for it, the consensus among psychiatrists seems to be that at least half of all *hikikomori* treat their parents with some type of violence" and in the summer of 2019 two separately gruesome *hikikomori* incidents were reported in Japan. The first involved the stabbing of 17 schoolgirls and two adults at a bus stop in Kawasaki by a purported *hikikomori* who later killed himself and, in a kind of twisted response, the second detailed a retired government official stabbing his own 44-year-old live-in son to death for fear of what he might do; "the father, 76, reportedly feared that his son, who had physically abused his mother, might attack others, specifically citing the mass stabbing in Kawasaki." For its part, the always-anonymous dregs of the so-called incel movement regularly invoke the names of incel mass-murderers Elliot Rodger and Alek Minassian when advocating violence against women or authority figures, their animus both alarming and deluded.

Further, being a product of self-absorbed "reject culture" gives *hikikomori* and incels their primary source of power. Binding the two disparate groups is a defeatist *we-don't-match-up-and-are-never-going-to-match-up* mentality. What's defeating them, then, isn't as important as the ultimate significance of the defeat. Having come out on the other side, the former *hikikomori* that tells Zielenziger that "the challenge is to preserve your inner feelings and unique identity while still finding a way to function in the larger world of the collective" articulates a way of being that is easy to identify but far harder to accomplish. Whether it's failing to attract a woman to date and have sex with or failing to match cultural and societal expectations, the obsession for incels and *hikikomori* alike revolves around failure, failure, failure. Via it each group's power, however reprehensible or misguided, is made manifest.

*

That year was one of just two seasons in Missouri. Heat so viscous that when you walked outside you wore it like a scarf that, triple-knit, draped down your torso and into your toes; cold that immediately formed icicles on your eyelashes if, indoors or out, you stopped moving for even a nanosecond. Relentless winter to endless summer, there seemed no grace period between shivering and sweating. Agitated, I stared at the flakes slowly descending en masse from the darkened sky, and I suffused into my skin the humidity molecules tormenting the bright blue air everywhere. The weather's new normal seemed to prophesy my own.

If that first involuntarily celibate year you'd asked me if I shared anything with either *hikikomori* or the incel movement I would have responded no, and that response would have been truthful. Yes, I isolated myself in my little physical and mental rooms and I stopped attempting to date. Yes, I glass half-emptied most situations I encountered, utilizing the full strength of my negative imaginative capabilities. And yes, I often played the self-absorbed victim, my problems the only ones that mattered.

What I didn't resign myself to, though, was failure, failure undeniable and everlasting. Instead I started reading Russian literature and going to therapy again.

*

More desirous of personal understanding, identity and security, Millennials become sexually active later in life and sleep with fewer people than their generational predecessors did, but conversely (and perhaps surprisingly) male Millennials are more prone to stereotypical masculinist attitudes than male members of the Baby Boomers or Generation X were. Titled "On Gender Differences, No Consensus on Nature vs Nurture" and using as its tagline the statement "Americans say society places a higher premium on masculinity than femininity," a 2017 Pew Research Center survey details how "Millennial men are far more likely than those in older generations to say men face pressure to throw a punch if provoked, join in when others talk about women in a sexual way, and have many sexual partners." The survey further discusses how, although only 24% of male Millennials classify themselves as "very masculine," many men of the Millennial generation nonetheless accord masculinity (and all its attendant attitudes and behaviors) substantial weight in their lives, with 82% of all men in the Millennial generation describing themselves as masculine to one degree or another, and just 18% abstaining from using the term as a self-descriptor.

*

It didn't cover male Millennials seeking or undergoing talk-therapy treatment, the "On Gender Differences" Pew survey, but by virtue of the minimalizing of forthright emotion that burrowing in one's masculinity can often beget, it has to be assumed that talking to a therapist isn't, for at least some substantial swath of men in the Millennial generation, the immediate go-to solution for mental health concerns. (As with everything, the Internet can tell you more if you're interested. Although their individual takes might be debatable, a quick Google search elicits articles with titles such as "Why Millennial Men Don't Go to Therapy: The most depressed generation won't get help despite having more access than ever before" and "Millennials are facing a mental health crisis, and it was entirely preventable.")

*

At the end of "Car Crash While Hitchhiking," the first story in Denis Johnson's collection *Jesus' Son*, the unnamed narrator, involved in the deathly crash but completely unscathed, tells a doctor imploring him to get checked out: "There's nothing wrong with me.'" Thinking back on the moment later, he relates, "There's nothing wrong with me"—I'm surprised I let those words out. But it's always been my tendency to lie to doctors, as if good health consisted only of the ability to fool them."

Most patients aren't in as dire straits as the narrator of "Car Crash While Hitchhiking," no. But due to embarrassment or fear of being judged, lying to one's doctor is prevalent in Western society. To be clear, these are often white lies, not life-threatening ones. Still, a white lie is a half-truth is a real fib.

*

Different than some of my male peers, I'd sought out therapy twice before in my life, at the ages of twenty-five and twenty-seven. Both times I'd found the experience frustrating. I'd talked, I'd listened, had worked on Rational Self-Management and the immediate recognizing and harnessing of my Automatic Negative Thoughts. Even so, nothing had really changed. Only talking to my therapists for a total of three hours a month and seeing each for, at most, four months at a time before abandoning everything hadn't helped. *That's like trying to cure a migraine by wrapping an Ace bandage tightly around your head and thinking happy, peaceful, anti-migraine thoughts* is how my friend V once described my therapeutic experience to me in an email. *You're not really doing anything and don't sound like you really want to do anything but by telling your therapist that you want to try you're trying to tell yourself. It sounds like a sort of lie* V wrote. Her mother having abandoned her family when she was three before later committing suicide when V was eight, V herself had been in therapy for years, with considerable success. *If you're willing, it can be there for you. But it's up to you, not the therapist.*

*

XIV. The easy attainment of love makes it of little value; difficulty of attainment makes it prized.

*

From the diaries of Cesare Pavese—25th December, 1937:

There is something sadder than growing old—remaining a child.

*

Back then I'd told my therapists I was insecure and left it at that. True, but only partway.

*

Older now and still searching, I aimed to lay it out, to not lie at all nor (consciously at least) self-aggrandize. Prudently or not, my guide here was the monologist Spalding Gray, whose work I'd discovered early in my Missouri sojourn and found revelatory for its insistence on interrogation and unvarnished directness of self.

*

Perishing by suicide in January 2004, in December 1985 Spalding Gray wrote:

"The whole process of writing… has been very healing, to the extent that it has projected into me a future. And although this cannot fully assure a future, it has at least created one for me to move toward, as I watch it race ahead before me."

*

And yet.

*

The first two therapists I found online, Googling "Blue Cross Blue Shield talk therapy coverage (sexuality self-esteem relationships)." The last I found by recommendation of a friend of a friend.

*

Both bespectacled married middle-aged straight white men from the Midwest, it is hard for me now to differentiate between those first two. Ted was #1, Steve was #2. Ted had slightly receding dusky blond hair, a penchant for wearing Crocs with socks, and a genial disposition that simultaneously soothed and irked me. Hair colored dusky blond also, Steve had a starchy crewcut gracelessly aspiring to fauxhawk, a penchant for wearing dark green V-neck sweaters, and a genial disposition that simultaneously soothed and irked me.

*

I laid it out as truthfully as possible, or at least tried to. I told TedSteve that I'd been celibate for a year and nine months, willfully for the first year but not for the last nine months. I told them that during that period I'd isolated myself and was very lonely. I told them that I didn't much care for the Midwest and how once I finished school I planned on leaving the area forever. I told them that I loved my family, my parents and younger brother, but felt somewhat distant from them emotionally. I told them that with new romantic partners I was always initially shy sexually, a so-called prude, and that sometimes that shyness overwhelmed my sense of sexual self both in the moment and down the line, months or even years later. I told them that, so far as I understood the word, I'd only been in love once, that it had been years ago, with a woman who broke up with me for someone older and more successful than me. I told them that, despite my intimacy issues or whatever you want to call them, I'd slept with multiple women, more, actually, than the national average for a man my age (did they by chance know the national average for a man my age?), and, in terms of prowess and proficiency, felt I was a serviceable lover, if somewhat unadventurous. I told them I wouldn't mind seeking out said adventure but wasn't sure, within the confines of my own present sexual machinery, how to do so. Spurious façade, I told them that I thought masculinity was a sham, but one I nevertheless felt inclined to live in. (Why?) Is it because I was so afraid of my masculinity that I felt intoxicated by that fear? I told them that going down on a woman sometimes felt shameful because it aroused me to such a degree, that I occasionally hesitated to do so because of my blood-red desire. I told them that even if I wasn't sure who I was from moment to moment, day to day, I often absorbedly lived inside my head to a probably unhealthy extent, and that this self-absorption seemed to be, for an aspiring writer at least, both problem and solution. I told them that the concept of lust as grief seemed to be a silly one to me. Walking back from the bar alone or driving my car next to the dense green empty cornfields everywhere around me, I couldn't help but believe in it nevertheless.

I told them that I loved to read but felt that sometimes I used this love as a way to mask my own personal feelings, sentiments and beliefs— repurposing the words and articulations of others as proxies or stand-ins for my own. I told them I had a robust scope of imagination, which both helped and hindered me. I told them I drank too much water and too much alcohol and that the former was contributing to my constant-micturition issues and the latter my depression. I told them that learning was important to me, perhaps *the* most important thing to me, but that with regards to academic learning specifically (at this point I'd been in the higher education system for nearly eight years) it was no doubt holding me back vis-à-vis the many societal fundaments and directives embedded in "the real world" that I still wasn't aware of or privy to. I told them if I was being honest with myself I tended to run from my problems rather than face them, that I moved around a lot as a result of this, that my geographical wanderlust no doubt had personal consequences for me. I told them that I was a very lucky person, incredibly privileged, and that I regularly forgot about this fact or downplayed it. I told them that the possibility of the private past becoming the public present scared and titillated me. I told them, repeatingly, above all else, that with so much "stuff" out there I wondered where my own "stuff" might one day soon or far fit in, and how a monastic life of quiet reflection seemed ideal and impossible to me. I told them that I felt like I was living inside a box of my own creation and that, although initially I had welcomed this, even luxuriated in it, now it felt like a trap. A la Spalding Gray I sometimes gesticulated wildly while conferring all of the above to TedSteve. At other times I stared at TedSteve's benignly shuffling feet or into TedSteve's four slowly blinking eyes.

*

Terminally unique, forever, shining star shining bright.

*

From the diaries of Cesare Pavese—29th August, 1944:

Only uniqueness justifies…the absolute value which puts us above all contingencies.

*

Perfect necessity. Eternally true.

*

TedSteve listened intently and took notes. They then asked me to do certain things: keep a gratitude journal; make a point of approaching one new person (man or woman) every day in order to start a casual, risk-free conversation with them. Take the time to identify my triggers (sexual and social) and, having done so, sort through each in the moment, thus allowing my (best) self the freedom to be who it could be without fear of personal persecution or censure. They asked me to conduct a daily mental inventory. Using transactional analysis, each worked with me on furthering my notions of personal autonomy and awareness.

At my request, TedSteve also recommended three books to me, *Sex Is Not a Natural Act and Other Essays* (1995) by Leonore Tiefer, *Neurosis and Human Growth: The Struggle Toward Self-Realization* (1950) by Karen Horney and *Loneliness: Human Nature and the Need for Social Connection* (2008) by John T. Cacioppo and William Patrick.

*

Although some of its Clinton Presidency era talking points now read a bit dated (the book was initially published in 1995, with a second edition coming out in 2004) and sentences such as "To understand sexual excitement, for example, you need to understand how psychology, biology and society interact and change" might stultify even potentially interested readers, psychiatrist and sex therapist

Leonore Tiefer's *Sex Is Not a Natural Act and Other Essays* was illuminating for me to encounter. Tiefer's primary concern in the book is with the social and cultural construction of sex; how our every understanding and insight of it has less to do with ancient biology and more to do with present day society. Sexual normality derives its purchase from the need for social conformity, and *Sex Is Not A Natural Act* takes its title from cultural theorist Raymond Williams's assertion that the word nature "is perhaps the most complex word in the [English] language." Every thought of *It's totally natural to want to* [*screw your beautiful girlfriend /screw your handsome boyfriend/ fight your worst enemy/ sleep until noon after a hard day's work/ dance naked at dawn on summer solstice/ ad infinitum*] deals, at its core, far more with social construction than any reasonable definition of naturality. In Tiefer's words, "Belief that sexuality comes naturally relieves our responsibility to acquire knowledge and make choices." She goes on to state:

"Natural sex, like a natural brassiere, is a contradiction in terms. The human sex act is a product of individual personalities, skills, and the scripts of our times. Like a brassiere, it shapes nature to something designed by human purposes and reflecting current fashion."

*

When asked if he worked from nature, meaning studying the world as represented in immaculately spruced trees and concentric pears and oranges in similarly concentric bowls, Jackson Pollock famously replied, "I am nature." What gets forgotten, however, is that it was the older artist Hans Hoffman—an Abstract Expressionist pioneer in his own right—who did the asking and, on hearing Pollock's reply, he retorted, "You don't work from nature, you work by heart. That's no good. You will repeat yourself."

Hoffman meant that, however natural a person or their art is, there's no getting away from the self's entanglement with society, that the more original one believes themselves to be the more they inevitably rely on ideas of originality that are tired and stale, unoriginal.

*

One of the standout tracks on their 1979 album *Entertainment!* (listed by *Rolling*

Stone at #483 in their 2009 "The 500 Greatest Albums of All Time" article), UK post-punk band Gang of Four's song "Natural's Not in It" calls for a renunciation of commodified societal constructions like Love and Pleasure and Sex. All discordant incision, Gang of Four's singer sing-shouts evocative enigmas like "The problem of leisure/ What to do for pleasure/ Ideal love a new purchase/ A market of the senses" and "Fornication makes you happy/ No escape from society/ Natural is not in it/ Your relations are of power" over jagged guitars and rapid-fire drum fills and breaks. Repeated six times, the chorus of "Natural's Not in It" is the lonely mantra "Repackaged sex your interest." The way Jon King, Gang of Four's singer, intones it again and again the listener feels indicted by association: Who hasn't had repackaged sex for mindless pleasure?

"The body is good business...This heaven gives me migraine" is how "Natural's Not in It" ends. King sings the words emphatically, but beneath there's a glimmer of indeterminacy. If humans can't allow themselves what they'd like to believe is non-negotiable "human nature," what are the consequences? There's no escape from society and the self within it, and King shouts against the mirage of naturality in rhythmic bursts and gasps. If natural's not in it, what is? Anything?

*

"I've got my hands on the one end/ And I don't know where to put them" The Promise Ring sings on "How Nothing Feels."

*

And yet.

*

In certain ways Tiefer's *Sex Is Not A Natural Act* dovetails with Michel Foucault's *The History of Sexuality*. (Tiefer's text is also indebted to the work of Eve Kosofsky Sedgwick, Judith Butler and Gayle Rubin, among other influential thinkers and theorists.) In that book Foucault writes, "The history of sexuality must first be written from the viewpoint of a history of discourses" and, although profoundly unsexy and unromantic, attempting to analyze those discourses beyond the world's 24-7 sexual arena might be the key to understanding one's own sexual self.

*

378 single-spaced pages and in my used copy every one of those pages aged a sallow yellow, I didn't actually read psychoanalyst Karen Horney's *Neurosis and Human Growth: The Struggle Toward Self-Realization.* The titles of some of the chapters seemed intriguing— "Alienation from Self;" "The Self-Effacing Solution: The Appeal of Love;" "Resignation: The Appeal of Freedom"—but when I actually tried to get through them I was at a loss. A Neo-Freudian and feminist, Horney took issue with some of Freud's primary theories—mainly in terms of gender, narcissism and sexuality—while agreeing with and elaborating on other central tenets made by the Austrian psychoanalyst.

The vast hallways of the Internet now tell me that *Neurosis and Human Growth* is Horney's major work and that it largely involves conceptions of the real self vs. the ideal self. The former is who we are, the latter who we want to be, and for neurotics the ideal self will, for various reasons, never be attainable. Horney refers to this phenomenon as "the tyranny of the should;" feeling that, for whatever reason, one *should* do a certain thing or *should* feel a certain way. According to Horney this tyranny forever divides the real self and the ideal one. For neurotics specifically, the unattainability of the ideal self brings out their latent inner critic and, ultimately, their self-hatred.

*

I is another.

*

I
Is
An
Other.

*

"I'm just variations on a theme" imparts eighty-year-old artist Ed Ruscha in a 2018 *Vanity Fair* feature article, neglecting to identify what that theme is, or its variations. The writer of the piece uses words like "endless" and "ineffable" and "cool" to describe him and his work, but Ruscha himself seems dubious, unwilling to commit to any pinned down definition, content not to know.

*

"There's never any center to it. No path, no line. There are great spaces where you pretend there used to be someone, but it's not true, there was no one" decrees Marguerite Duras in *The Lover.*

Wandering, her nameless protagonist never finds him either. The easiest way of consoling oneself in terms of this absence is to say that it's the searching that matters more: centers do not hold but the spaces around them that we eventually find ourselves occupying offer respite and, hopefully, firm ground to stand on. But both Duras and her protagonist know better. No path, no line.

*

Between the pages of 13-112, sentences highlighted by a previous owner in green ink in my used copy of *Neurosis and Human Growth: The Struggle Toward Self-Realization:*

In a healthy human relationship the moves toward, against, or away from others are not mutually exclusive.

Self-idealization always entails a general self-glorification, and thereby gives the individual the much needed feeling of significance and superiority over others.

And as we lose the neurotic obsession with self, as we become free to grow ourselves, we also free ourselves to love and to feel concern for other people.

The actual, empirical self becomes the offensive stranger to whom the idealized self happens to be tied, and the latter turns against the stranger with hate and contempt. The actual self becomes the victim of the proud idealized self.

*

Between the pages of 13-112, sentences highlighted by a previous owner in blue ink:

The neurotic's egocentricity is built on an entirely different and much more complicated base. He is consumed with himself because he is driven by his psychic needs, torn by his conflicts, and compelled to adhere to his peculiar solutions.

The second characteristic inherent in all the elements of the search for glory is the great and peculiar role *imagination* plays in them...But imagination may be productive or unproductive: it can bring us closer to the truth of ourselves—as it often does in dreams—or carry us far away from it.

The more injurious work of imagination concerns the subtle and comprehensive distortions of reality he is not aware of fabricating.

The more his irrational imagination has taken over, the more likely he is to be positively horrified at anything that is real, definite, concrete, or final.

*

"It is my daimon if there ever was one" imparts Mary Ruefle in *On Imagination,* speaking on all the nefarious ways that the imagination can bring the truth of ourselves into certain unproductive tinges of light. Stark cold fictional facts.

*

Between the pages of 13-112, sentences written by an unknown hand in the margins in red ink:

Through imagination life is better?

You idolize yourself b/c of the lack of self finding

Confused by his own emotions he does not know who he is / no longer has control/ he is controlled

*

Between the pages of 13-112, sentences written by a different unknown hand in the margins in black ink:

failure to love determines his qualities

Where are we?

*

Between the pages of 113-378, nothing is written in the margins and, green ink, only one passage is highlighted:

If he can muster and maintain an attitude of "don't care," he feels less bothered by his inner conflicts and can attain a semblance of inner peace. Since he can do this only by resigning from active living, "resignation" seems a proper name for this solution. It is in a way the most radical of all solutions and, perhaps for this very reason, most often procures conditions that allow for a fairly smooth functioning. And, since our sense of what is healthy is generally blunted, resigned people often pass for "normal."

*

I'm still reading John T. Cacioppo and William Patrick's book *Loneliness: Human Nature and the Need for Social Connection*. Whether they realize it or not, most people that I know are reading it too.

*

TedSteve helped me and to state otherwise would be a lie. Under their care I felt more willing to accept my self, whoever that self actually was or could be. The books they recommended helped and keeping a gratitude journal helped and working on identifying and acting on my anxiety-inducing triggers helped. On TedSteve's recommendation, making a concerted effort to go up to more people with a friendly word or face helped.

*

I stopped seeing Ted after five months. I stopped seeing Steve after four months.

*

Despite the fact that I'd never been a person who relied on in-the-moment intuition—*Your first thought is almost never your best thought* I'd tell my writing students over and over again in a strident voice—my reasons for quitting therapy with TedSteve were based on nebulous perceptions and understandings. I stopped because I could. No one could hold me accountable except my self, and I just didn't wanna go anymore. Thoughtless as that.

*

One of my own definitions of prudery entails refusing to help oneself out of fear, insecurity or misunderstanding. Prudery as weapon, bared and brandished against the self.

*

So I stewed in my subversion. Happiness was a river and, even if I sometimes swam in it, I swam in it alone. At the time I was reading the New York School poets—namely Barbara Guest, James Schuyler and Kenneth Koch—and, from his poem "Days and Nights," I kept a line of Kenneth Koch's in my head: "I have never been inspired by sex, always by love." Not in love and not having sex, this line nevertheless inspired me. It enabled me to believe that the life I was living wasn't a lie of my own creation. Or, if it was, it was the fabrication that I wanted to live.

*

From the diaries of Cesare Pavese—5th January, 1938:

The art of living is the art of knowing how to believe lies. The fearful thing about it is that, not knowing what truth may be, we can still recognize a lie.

*

Even lying to my involuntarily celibate self, though, I couldn't make it quite work. Four months after I stopped seeing Steve I began to think about therapy again, only this time I asked friends if they might have anyone to recommend. At that point I'd been celibate for over two years. That didn't matter, though. What mattered was how emotionally stunted I felt to romantic affection of any kind. (Let alone feelings of love.) In the past when I masturbated—which I was now doing occasionally, semi-occasionally, regularly, often—it had always been nostalgically, to memories of former lovers. I might have watched porn to incite my exterior lust, but in my head I was thinking of my past partners and my past selves at our most intimate and tender moments together.

*

Written in 1916-1917 but not actually published until 1972, in his *Memoirs*, William Butler Yeats writes:

"I was tortured by sexual desire and had been for many years. I have often said to myself that someday I would put it all down in a book that some young man of talent might not think as I did that my shame was mine alone...Normal sexual intercourse does not affect me more than other men, but [mastrubation], though never frequent, was plain ruin."

And then, in a later chapter:

"It was a time of great personal stsrain and sorrow. Since my mistress had left me, no other woman had come into my life, and for nearly seven years none did. I was tortured by sexual desire and disappointed love. Often as I walked in the woods at Coole it would have been a relief to have screamed aloud. When desire became an unendurable torture, I would mastrubate, and that, no matter how moderate I was, would make me ill. It never occurred to me to seek another love."

*

Plain ruin. Tortured.

*

Now, however, I banished all thoughts of yesteryear. I simply watched the computer screen and rampantly reacted to what I saw with my hand. The release was the same but how I got there had changed. A resignation had descended that would have worried me if I'd noticed. I didn't notice. After leaving the bar alone on Friday nights I stared at the screen and didn't wish I was elsewhere, with someone else. I didn't notice.

*

Most of my friends didn't have a therapist to recommend. Most of them weren't in therapy. Except one of my better female friends, K, who'd off and on seen a woman named Larissa for the past year. *She's definitely not for everyone* K told me by way of endorsement. *She's a widower and will tell you about it. She has a daughter that I don't think she's in touch with. And she has this weird thing about the phrase "self-care." But I can say that she's helped me out with stuff. She's pretty good.*

*

On the basis of that testimonial from K I bit, more out of curiosity about Larissa as a personality than in a desire to find effective therapeutic treatment. I Googled Larissa, called her and left a voicemail. Two hours later she called back when I was out walking my dog, left me a voicemail. On her message her voice was mild, gentle; it seemed a voice entirely befitting a therapist. When I called her back again and we actually spoke the voice was the same, a deferential probe regarding what I was seeking help with and what times would be good to meet for a consultation. Albeit vaguely so, I told her my situation and at the end of our conversation Larissa asked how I had found her. *Online* I said. *And my friend K told me about you.* I expected a short pause, a searching for remembrance followed by some type of generalized affirmation: *Yes, I enjoyed working with K! or K—of course! Please tell her hello for me, will you?* But Larissa only—and immediately—said *K.* It was a definitive response, end-stopped, without hint of a question. Then came a long pause, two beats later than I expected. *She's one of my close friends* I said, silence-stifling. *That's great* Larissa said, voice and tone an evasion (masking) of what it had been at the beginning of the call. After making plans to see Larissa the following week, I hung up somewhat mystified and texted K. *When you were seeing that therapist Larissa, did things end badly between you two? Or why did you stop seeing her? I'm meeting her next week.* K texted back several hours later, insouciantly and indirect: *No, she's great. That'll be good that you're going.* I replied a few minutes later: *And?* K didn't respond, a thing not entirely out of character for her—she was nearing the end of writing her dissertation on the role the female hand plays in Victorian literature and text messages are text messages—but it still caused me to wonder.

*

I pictured a woman looking like Lydia Davis or Anne Carson. Thin, petite, unassuming in a slightly enigmatic way. A taut listener with pert ears, the sound of her voice a reasonable reproduction of her face and body.

A couch, two love seats and an orderly wooden desk nestled off to the corner, stage right, same as TedSteve had had, I pictured a clean nondescript room in a nondescript building populated by numerous clean nondescript rooms, most filled by other therapists or mental health practitioners of one variety or other.

*

The room Larissa practiced in, then, proved to largely match my prediction. It was clean and nondescript, stationed in a drab 4-story building adjacent to a strip mall. There was a small couch that she sat on and a comfortable upright lounger chair that I sat on. Larissa's office, though, carried a certain subtle expectancy within it, one that had not been present in TedSteve's, nor in any other therapist space I'd ever entered. Non-bodily presence that seemed to yet preside in ironclad abstractions like Truth and Fear and Hope, abstractions strangely turned actual and existent every time I passed through the doorway. Fully present, engaged and anxious, driving to see Larissa always made me feel like I was driving to see my therapist, which I was.

With regards to her actual person, however, and my stereotypical (racist?) therapist assumptions about it, Larissa proved to be *very* different. Biracial, her father was a white Korean War veteran, her mother a Korean woman considerably younger than her father. Larissa was also big. Tall, just one or two inches shorter than my 6'1. Additionally, she was rotund, thirty pounds or so overweight. Upon meeting her she intimidated me in a way that TedSteve hadn't. When we shook hands, hers were not soft. Wrinkle-less and callous-free, they were finely contoured and firm and strong and heavy.

I don't remember that first meeting with Larissa well. Or I remember it extremely well; it's only that the memory I have deals less in sounds, smells and images and more in grey and beige swathes of clammy feeling. Not just looking at the Rothko painting but living inside it, unable to get out.

When I'd first met TedSteve I'd laid out my "case" for them and both had, by the end of our first consultation, accepted that I was a flawed individual, one that they desired to help. With Larissa, however, a brisk incomprehension settled itself into the room midway through our initial encounter. I was about a fourth of the way through my long, self-involved description of why I was there and what I was seeking out of therapy—the words *celibate* and *prudery* and *sex* had been mentioned several times, as well as *lost, loneliness, lack* and *masculine*—when Larissa abruptly cut me off in the middle of a short and what I thought focused tangent on why I couldn't seem to meditate, even though it would no doubt greatly help me with everything. *It's just that, you know, when I get into the position or whatever and close my eyes I—*

From behind her glasses Larissa looked out at me impassively, then said *I don't think I can help you.* I looked at her quizzically. *With meditation?* She shook her head. *With any of it.* Having never been rejected by a therapist before and not sure if that was what was happening, I stayed quiet, staring at her. Seeing that she was entirely content in the silence, I finally asked *Well, what do you do? Who do you—I mean, online it said—* Again Larissa cut me off, this time by standing up and walking over to her desk to grab a stick of lip balm. She gingerly applied it to her lips and walked back to the couch in one fluid motion.

I can't recall what she said next, not exactly. Up to that point I'd been used to my every mental health professional being off-limits about their own life. They'd tell me their backgrounds and histories briefly, but the onus had always been on me, not them. If I pried, which I did on occasion, they would state the vague contours: *we've been lovingly married for 13 years, yes, lovingly all the while.* Or *our dog died after a long illness, yes, cancer, yes, but it'd been something that we were prepared for, had seen coming, and, anyway, let's get back to you, to what you said before about—*

This formula, then, had suited me. I'd been of the understanding that cognitive behavioral therapy was primarily an activity where I talked, the therapist listened, and then clarities would materialize in the air by virtue of this talking/listening dynamic. If this had never really worked in the past didn't preclude the possibility that it would in the future. Right?

*

It was a silence I would soon get used to, sometimes even bask in. This time, though, we sat in it and I felt an annoyance rapidly scaling towards anger, even revulsion. *Who the fuck,* I thought, *was this overweight motherfucker with dark rings under her eyes and a shitty fucking waiting room filled with stupid obligatory issues of* ***TIME*** *and* ***National Geographic*** *that dumb people read dully with vapid eyes, hoping to forget. Her too tightly laced and too brightly white New Balances, her unfurrowed brow burrowed into her eyebrows, her sundress and her fucking silence,* *who the fuck—*

Larissa was intently staring at me. *I'd like to ask about your teeth* she said. *What?* I said. *Your teeth. Do you brush regularly? Do you floss? Have you ever had problems with your teeth in any way?* Hate is too strong a word, but I've never cared for Mark Rothko's paintings because I often don't know what to do with them, especially after leaving the darkened gallery. Flat squares unto dense color fields, they're fine to look at and easy to forget.

No, not really I said, my voice brittle. *When I was younger, like elementary school, I used to get cavities because my parents had different schedules and I ate too much candy while they were gone, but now I'm pretty good.* Another short pause. *Well, that's a plus* Larissa said lightly, her face giving no clues. I was beginning to settle into my hatred for her. *What does that have to do with* I started to say, but once more I was cut off. *I used to have a lot of problems with my own teeth that were actually symptomatic of more deeply rooted issues.* I didn't know where she was going with this and didn't care. But I sat there not speaking, not rolling my eyes, blank look on my face hopefully masking my inner seethe.

I used to brush my teeth a lot. A lot a lot, three times a day, sometimes even four. It was another way to succeed, the easiest way. I'm not an only child—I have an older sister—but when I was a freshman in high school she was already gone and the legacy had already been set, straight A's, 4.0 GPA, the works. My sister's smart and she studied. She got good grades. So did I but there were only two of us and by the time she was gone I'd been established as more of the fuckup. I was fatter. I dyed my hair. We probably had the same number of friends but mine were—have you seen the movie **The Breakfast Club**? Even though I had, I spitefully shook my head no. *Well, it's—you said you were thirty-one—before your time. It doesn't matter.*

What I'm getting at it is I didn't brush my teeth so much because I was looking for a release or because I was acting out. It just felt good to do it. And I liked it doing it. After the first thirty seconds my gums would start to bleed and that would be what I wanted. I'd keep brushing and when I spit blood back into the sink it felt like I'd accomplished something. Larissa paused, studying her hands before staring at me dead set again. *But I was wearing down the enamel on my teeth and my gums were receding to the point that if I lifted my upper lip I could see the recession. Really gross. When I forgot to completely wash it down one day my mom found the bathroom sink partially filled with blood and I was at the dentist's office the next morning. Since I was young they were really concerned about the gum recession, if it'd become permanent.*

Another pause. *Did it?* I asked, my voice betraying interest even if outwardly I tried to maintain my façade of pissy indifference. *Oh yes. Definitely. You can still see the grooves.* Yet again she paused. *But nothing too bad in the end. Gums grow back if you let them.* I wasn't sure where we were or how we got there. *Did you stop because you had to or because you wanted to?* I asked, now making no attempt to mask my engagement with her story.

Because I had to. I never wanted to. Only now I have an electric toothbrush and watch the mirror when I brush she said, smiling, the first time she'd really done so. I smiled too, but a moment later we were back where we started. Noticing my discomfort, Larissa glanced at me evenly. *I bring up teeth because earlier you mentioned sex and masculinity and some societal expectations. You also said that you were aware of your own self-absorption and childish thoughts. That it's not about having sex or desiring it; it's about your own insecurity and apprehension. So it sounds to me like you already know the issues you face, which is a good thing. But if you're aware of all that and feel confident that it sums up the reasons why you came to see me, we're at the end rather than the beginning. Self-esteem is something that's earned. And I simply can't give it to you, even if you come here every week and I pile on the*—she raised her fingers in air quotes— *"self-care" exercises. When I was brushing my teeth so hard that my gums would bleed and I would spit blood into the sink I didn't know why I was doing it; I only knew that it felt good. Most people who come to see me are like that. They know the changes they want to make but don't know how to get there. It sounds like you think you know both, though—the changes and how to achieve them. I mean, inferiority complexes are—if sleeping with a woman first thing is something that you truly think will—*

Well, you cut me off before I said, cutting her off, hating her, my cheeks flushed, my eyes beady and narrowed into iris-flagrant ovals. *That's not really what I said, not at all.* Larissa stared at me. *What I said was that I actually have a really healthy amount of self-esteem but that I sometimes just get stuck in these negative self-defeating thought patterns that fuck with me. I get in my head and I can't stop.* She was still staring, barely blinking, not saying anything. *I believe you* she finally said, her look that of a textbook unbeliever. I expected her to go on but that it was it and moments later I was walking out of her office, with no second appointment scheduled. I couldn't wait to not see her again. Walking to my car I was already texting my friend K how wrong she'd been in recommending Larissa to me.

*

Couldn't wait to never see her again. When I talked to K about it face to face later in the week—she hadn't texted me back— she was again evasive, saying nothing more than *I didn't like her at first either.* Even when I pressed her further K wouldn't elaborate except to reiterate *She's not for everyone. I told you that.*

*

Couldn't wait.

*

The first two stanzas of Anne Carson's poem "My Religion" read:

"My religion makes no sense
and does not help me
therefore I pursue it.

When we see
how simple it would have been
we will thrash ourselves.

*

In "Idle," the first section of Lydia Davis's short story "What You Learn About the Baby," Davis writes:

It is easy to do nothing and become impatient. It is not easy to do nothing and not mind it, not mind the hours passing, the hours of the morning passing and then the hours of the afternoon, and one day passing and the next passing, while you do nothing.

*

A distinct childhood memory of mine: everywhere yellow, in front and above and to the sides great oil slicks of yellow, and me staring up in wonder, my crib containing me physically but my mind endeavoring to will its way out somehow. Barely aware of my hands and legs or their actualities of usage but sensing it all somewhere in my head and staring into the dense yellow color field around me, waiting for I knew not what.

*

Religion of the self and the child an adult that can't stop trying to attain a version of personhood that, Peter Pan-like, finds a home in what will never be, what once was and is no longer. But still trying; Neverland of one.

*

A month and a half later, still celibate, still the same, I was back in Larissa's office, having scheduled an appointment as an act of personal defiance. Perhaps what I needed out of therapy wasn't what I wanted out of it. Tough love, radical honesty, blah blah blah. I was tired of being stuck in a version of myself that I couldn't seem to comprehend. Or relinquish.

When I'd called to make the appointment Larissa hadn't seem surprised to hear from me and after a brief talk about my goals (happiness, generally, sexually or both; some type of contentment, however fleeting) we started where we'd left off before, only this time Larissa seemed more open, less intimidating and aloof. Talking to her without reservation, I resolved to let my mind crack open as wide as possible.

That second appointment with Larissa began the template of all the thrice-a-month meetings with her that I would have over the next ten months. Sitting down in the lounger chair, I would attempt to explain what I was feeling and why. Larissa would listen carefully. Having done so she would then proceed to tell me (occasionally using anecdotes from her own life) why what I was so worked up about didn't much matter: Most people, especially those from Western cultures, are pathologically self-centered; why did I think I was so special in terms of that obsession? (No one is terminally unique, no one.) Self-pity is the main sign of selfishness and further just not a very good look, especially if one is hoping to attract friends or lovers. Loneliness is part of life and it can be an exceptionally fulfilling part if you let it. Just don't allow it to be the only part. Love will happen or it won't and if it doesn't it doesn't; you keep up regardless. You reject unhelpful nihilism at all costs, reject mistrust. You allow yourself to be vulnerable. You refuse to be self-indulgent and to *not* be self-indulgent.

And as for all this talk about shyness and being a prude? Unless it constituted an inclination or way of being that I wanted to embody or accept—which was perfectly fine if that was the case—it represented too many self-defeating prophecies. Did I truly believe that everyone else out there was having romping, euphoric, confident and assertive sex all the time with every partner? I'd talked with my friends, I'd read too much, I knew that wasn't case. The problem with boxing oneself in, Larissa let me know, is the box. Always too many blackened corners and never enough opportunities for basking in the light. (How baskings differ from blindings in every which way.) Here Larissa would invariably quote Yogi Berra, with her favorite two quotes being *If the world were perfect, it wouldn't be* and *Don't worry about making too many wrong mistakes.* She recited each of these somewhat at random and when she did so I was never actually sure why, whether it was because they seemed to contextually fit with what I was discussing or whether she'd instead just grown bored with my present soliloquy.

*

TedSteve and the therapists I'd seen when I was younger had all encouraged me to read widely and to jot down my thoughts as often as possible. Gratitude journals, sure, but also any kind of reading and writing was considered a good thing in their eyes. Disciple of the written word, particularly when it was imaginatively rendered, I was only too happy to oblige.

A few months into my treatment, however, Larissa stated that all this reading and writing was detracting from self-discovery rather than prodding me towards it. Such activities were too insular, too introspective. *That's* where all this inappropriately intimate talk was coming from, this incessant reading. It's all too much overthinking and analyzing. *If you're going to read,* Larissa said one day, *read Russian literature. Read Tolstoy, Chekhov, Dostoevsky. They knew what living and wanting and suffering meant.* When, after some back and forth, I was forced to inform Larissa that such a statement was dripping with I'm-getting-an-A-in-11th-grade-AP-English-class-cliché, she only shrugged. *You need to worry less about reading and more about the world outside your head. You said it yourself—the imagination plays tricks and where has it gotten you anyway.*

*

In one of the more memorable exchanges with his psychiatrist Dr. Jennifer Melfi, New Jersey gangster Tony Soprano equates successful mental health treatment with successful defecation. "You know sometimes what happens in here is like taking a shit," he says, sighing, his face heavy. "Yes, okay," Melfi responds. "Although I prefer to…think of it…more like childbirth." Tony can't see it. "Trust me," he says immediately. "It's like taking a shit."

The Sopranos being one of her favorite shows, Larissa relayed that anecdote to me gleefully. *That's the way it really is* she said.

*

"...when you can't talk, reality comes rushing in on you very strongly" is how Spalding Gray puts it in his piece "47 Beds." Listening to Larissa talk about her own life, this is something that I learned subconsciously. She never got into name-and-date specifics, but Larissa would talk and sometimes *talk* and while doing so I learned things about my own self. Unlike my friend K, I didn't glean anything about Larissa's relationship with her daughter or deceased husband, although I was told that the latter figure had died suddenly and unexpectedly, during a period of separation between the two.

But I did find out Larissa's favorite video game (World of Warcraft), favorite color (forest green, same as mine), favorite yoga pose (the Bridge) and why she became a therapist (to help people, sure, but also, at least initially, to work with others on her own insecurity and inadequacy issues). She hated the phrase "self-care" because it implied that people shouldn't care about themselves all the time, that "self-care" was something to press on and off again like a button. (To be honest, I never fully understood this pet peeve of hers.) Larissa obliquely implied that her relationship with her parents had always been emotionally distant and that the more weight she tried to lose the more she failed to lose it. Although Larissa did not delve into those aspects of her life with me, when I talked about my own sexual and romantic successes and failures I felt like a conversation was happening between us. That, unlike with previous therapists, I wasn't baring my proverbial soul against so many silent, meaningless nods and murmurs of assent. In the last months of my seeing her even when Larissa said nothing it had the power of feeling like she divulged to me some subtle nugget of profundity. Which is what I needed: to be heard, advised and counseled, yes, but also to be made to feel like what I was saying didn't matter nearly as much as I thought it did. Everyone's a prude at times, shy and unsure. Everyone succeeds at failure. Thing full of anxious fear, love is all that the poets proselytize and the lost and lonely lament. Larissa talked or Larissa listened and I began to slowly accept a fuller, less involved version of my self in the process.

*

And yet.

*

IV. It is well-known that love is always increasing or decreasing and this is especially the case when dealing with one's own myriad self.

*

From the diaries of Cesare Pavese—18th December, 1937:

There is something even sadder than falling short of one's own ideals: to have realized them.

In understanding what Pavese means here, I have on sunnier days the wherewithal to disagree with him. And when it rains I survey the sky for the cracks of light that I know will soon rainbow through.

*

In a way that I never had previously, I started remembering my dreams soon after I began seeing Larissa. They were all fairly standard and would have no doubt bored Freud: only needing one more class to graduate high school or college and not being, for unknown reasons, allowed to take it, walking lost down a cavernous hallway, unsure where I was headed or why. A recurring dream about either falling or being trapped in some kind of pulsating Blade Runneresque oil well; every time I had this dream I woke with a start. Reminiscent of a classic *The Twilight Zone* episode, boarding a transatlantic flight just so I could read my favorite book (which book was never clear) and upon takeoff realizing I'd left the book at home, that all was for naught and I was stuck flying alone to a place I didn't want to go. Involving former girlfriends or would-be girlfriends, there were sexual dreams as well, each of which ended the way all sex dreams end: unsatisfactorily, still full of desire.

When over the course of my seeing her I told Larissa about each of these dreams she wasn't impressed, beyond commenting on the fact that if I hadn't been able to remember my dreams before seeking her care something about what we were doing in therapy was having an impact. I agreed, although I told Larissa that, even if I was curious what she thought about them, I'd never been a fan of Freud and dream interpretation. *Freud didn't invent dreams. Or interpretation* she said by way of a response, and when I pressed her as to her own opinion on the renowned German psychoanalyst she only quoted Yogi Berra: *In baseball, you don't know nothing*. I left it at that.

*

All of the Russian authors Larissa recommended to me I'd read at one point or another, but I went back, checking short story collections by Chekhov and Tolstoy out from the library and digging up my own copy of *The Gambler* by Dostoevsky. As I read I wasn't sure what I was looking for and at times I felt like the overachieving honors student that I'd never actually been. That each 19th century writer had something to tell me about suffering, selfhood and sexuality I didn't doubt, but being that Larissa hadn't insisted on my reading—she wanted me to go out into the world rather than bookly shy away from it—meant that I jumped around with abandon, beginning some stories in the middle and, growing bored, not finishing. Others I read backwards, starting at the end. A completist by nature, front to back, this seemed like the best way to read wrongly and I succeeded at it. Chekhov in particular I flitted around in, moving from the sordid mental institution in "Ward No. 6" to the existential religiosity of "The Black Monk" in a non-linear matter of minutes. My only divergence from this errancy came in the form of two short stories by Tolstoy and *The Gambler* by Dostoevsky, all of which I read in full.

Although my reading method was my own, I felt confident that it would teach me what I needed to know. Which it did, but in a way that I could not have foreseen. The starting point, I learned, matters far less than the order in which things make sense.

*

"Confidence does not become me" writes Cyril Connolly in *The Unquiet Grave*. He's indulging his insecurity, yes, but he's also asserting his own peculiar sense of exceptionality, one that most people would rather bury deep inside themselves than flaunt openly.

*

Entails coming to terms with Connolly's uncomfortableness with confidence, one of my own definitions of prudery. And then, in a tempest of resolve, suddenly breaking free and pushing through the walls of the box until daylight floods the darkness and, awestruck, the self is momentarily still stuck in place.

*

Written during a period of his life when he had come to believe that teaching and education were far more important than art or creative writing, Tolstoy's stories "The Kreutzer Sonata" and "The Devil" are lustful repudiations of sex and sexuality, with the protagonist in each suffering from a desire that drives him mad; in the face of sexual temptation, all personal selfhood and freedom is lost.

Banned for a period of years by the U.S. Post Office (in translation or otherwise, no mail carrier was allowed to distribute it) due to its lurid depiction of sex, "The Kreutzer Sonata" is the worse story of the two. Taking the form of a didactic train-car confession between an older man, Pozdnyshev, who previously murdered his wife when he found out about her affair, and an unnamed younger man solely existing to hear Pozdnyshev's tale, "The Kreutzer Sonata" hits the reader hard in the face with themes of Christian morality, misogyny and general chasteness celebration. After having five children with her, Pozdnyshev (always conflicted about the sexual act, which isn't to say that, from his prostitute-seeking youth to his status as a married, virile adult man, he ever stopped having sex) begins to see his unhappy marriage for what it is once his unnamed wife starts to use birth control and her having more children is out of the question. Hating himself and using sex with his wife as a self-flagellating means of acting out his shame, Pozdnyshev eventually stabs his better half to death when he finds her (fully clothed) with a violinist named Trukhachevsky. In an unsurprising twist at the story's end, he's eventually acquitted of his crime due to the suspicion of an affair between the two.

Because it turns a person into an unthinking animal, Pozdnyshev believes that sex is unnatural, that the virginal state in a woman is her highest accomplishment. For Pozdnyshev love is loathsome and swinish, yet it is something he seems to have no power to act against. In fact, to love is no different than to hate. Discussing the state of his relationship with his wife midway through the story, Pozdnyshev observes: "We didn't understand than that this love and anger were one and the same animal feeling, only from different ends." One of those ends, then, eventually allows Pozdnyshev to cold-bloodedly murder his wife, his lover, mother of his five sainted children.

*

In the famous opening to his *A Lover's Discourse: Fragments*, Roland Barthes writes, "The necessity for this book is to be found in the following consideration: that the lover's discourse is today *of an extreme solitude*."

This is Pozdnyshev's view also, although how he reacts to such isolation is decidedly problematic. Even with all the sex he has had in the past, Pozdnyshev is perhaps the first incel, the first box man to get stuck inside the box with no hope of finding a way out.

*

"I let my memories fall through/ It's not my fault/ I blame my sexuality" Daddy

Issues sings on "I'm Not."

*

Although different in form and tone than "The Kreutzer Sonata," Tolstoy's "The Devil" presents a somewhat similar scenario. Tormentedly in love with his wife Liza, who has recently given birth to their first child, young wealthy landowner Evgeny cannot forget the lusty passion he had before he was married with Stepanida, a peasant woman who still lives on his large estate. Not being able to get Stepanida out of his mind, he shoots himself in the head at the end of the story and the problem is thus solved. Or he doesn't shoot himself, he shoots Stepanida instead— "The Devil" was not published in Tolstoy's lifetime and the work has two endings, the first completed with a suicide, the second with a homicide. Regardless of the conclusion, though, both versions of "The Devil" end (with the exception of a short acknowledgement of Evgeny's murder in the homicidal version) the same way:

"And indeed, if Evgeny Irtenev was mentally ill, then all people are just as mentally ill, and the most mentally ill are undoubtedly those who see signs of madness in others that they do not see in themselves."

*

Desire as mental illness, as a pestilence that blankets the landscape with its bounty.

*

XX. A man in love is always apprehensive.

*

"Love is a thing full of anxious fear," especially when it seems there is no way out of it. Entrenched by love, locked down by it, smothered and suffocating.

*

When I tried to talk to Larissa about "The Kreutzer Sonata" and "The Devil" she claimed ignorance, telling me she hadn't read either. *I hope you're reading those out at a coffeeshop and not in the basement of your house though* is all she deigned to offer.

*

I *had* been reading them in my basement, where I had my office.

*

And yet.

*

On the third morning of reading Dostoevsky's *The Gambler* at the downtown coffeeshop I'd begun stationing myself at after Larissa's exhortation, I saw M. We hadn't set eyes on one other since our final failed date eighteen months earlier. She looked noticeably older and more composed to me, the lines in her face lovingly grooved in by time's surrender. No fanny pack anymore but an over the shoulder book bag with the words *NO NRML FUTURE* emblazoned on it in neon green bubble type, hair still strawberry blond but darker now and, pixie-perfect, cut shorter.

Staring at her and trying to hide it, M saw me and came immediately over, as if we'd just parted ways a week before. *So what are you reading?* she said, her voice assured, her hands reaching out for my book in the same melodic harmony as her body sitting down on the chair across from me. *Actually, I didn't know that you knew how to read. Is this just for show? Are you secretly plotting some type of covert mission here and this*—she glanced at the title—*The Gambler is your cover? Most Americans deep-down actually envy those Russian spies, you know.* For a long baffled second I stared at her, then came to my senses and nodded. *My code name is Herbie and my safety word is Patriot. This whole silly life I've led, it's all been an elaborate ruse up until this moment.*

*

The oft-quoted beginning to Duras's *The Lover*:

"I've known you for years. Everyone says you were beautiful when you were young, but I want to tell you I think you're more beautiful now than then. Rather than your face as a young woman, I prefer your face as it is now. Ravaged."

It's the narrator's lover talking to her years later, of course, but it's also the most perfect and deadening once-upon-a-time tale ever told, the tatters it begins with the same ones still found fraying at the book's end. In ending, love begins again. And ends. And—

*

Still a flight attendant and visual artist, M was now thinking about her next steps, what did she actually want to do with her life and where did she want to do it. New York was too expensive but New York, or possibly New Orleans or Santa Fe or Seattle or Northern California or Chicago. But for now she was back in Missouri, on an indefinite furlough, working on her upcoming gallery show at Bauer. What about me though—was I done with school or nearly so and how was my own work and where, anyway, was the best place to get burritos now in this godforsaken town?

We talked in the coffeeshop for an hour, M and I, then made plans to meet at a bar the next night. In the course of our conversation I told her that all was going swimmingly for me, that I was luxuriating in the moment while grabbing at the future with confident hands, balanced breath.

*

From the diaries of Cesare Pavese—3rd February, 1941:

Basically, the secret of life is to act as though we possessed the thing we most painfully lack... The comfort of this vision lies in believing it, not in whether it is real.

*

After M came back to my place that next night and we slept together, but before we slept together again the next morning, I asked her what she'd thought of me previously, those eighteen months back. Not a mincer of words, she responded *I thought you were someone who was pretty taken with your ability to play hard to get. And that you were shy and insecure but also kind of...macho about it I guess.* Never having heard the word used before in reference to me, I was surprised. *What do you mean macho?* M thought for a second. *Like you had what was a real badass secret that everyone wanted to know. I don't know... no offense but I didn't really think about you very much when I was in and out of town these past couple years.*

*

One of the author's minor works, *The Gambler* by Dostoevsky is about an introspective roulette-addicted neurotic named Alexei who is hopelessly immersed in a doomed-to-fail love triangle. Passionate and fiery, his life is all or nothing, no middle ground. Walking into a casino for the first time in his life early in the novella he states:

> ...probably I had felt for a long time already that I would leave Roulettenburg a different man and that something was about to happen which would radically and irrevocably change my life. I felt that it was bound to happen. Although it may seem ridiculous to say that I expected so much from roulette, I find the generally accepted opinion that it is stupid to expect anything from gambling even more ridiculous. And why should gambling be considered worse than any other way of getting money, such as commerce, for instance? It's true, of course, that out of a hundred persons who play roulette, perhaps one winds up a winner. But why should I care about that?

*

By the end of the book, though, Alexei cares more than he would have ever thought possible. What began as a way of thought turned into a way of life. Down to his last dollar before heading back into the casino again and winning it all back ten times over, the future is the past ad infinitum. "Tomorrow, tomorrow, it will all be over!" is the last sentence of *The Gambler*, Alexei's plea already abandoned before it even leaves his mouth. Tomorrow will come; nothing will change.

*

M and I started dating, casually at first and then more seriously. I tried not to overintellectualize it, tried not to let my imagination throttle into overdrive. The happy accident of our meeting and how we were both uncertain of where our futures would take us. The instant, effortless rapport between us and how simply and easily our bodies in bed seemed to maneuver equally into position. When, after the first time, I told M that what had just happened between us hadn't happened between me and anyone else in three years, she just smiled, nodded her head. *No words* she said, tracing over my eyebrows and closed eyes with both of her hands.

*

For Roland Barthes, falling in love is nothing more than the existence of signs. (In this regard he is no different than Andreas Capellanus, Stendhal or Neil Strauss.) In heat, the lover sees untold significance where anyone else would merely see randomness or chaos. Barthes writes that every lover "...creates meaning, always and everywhere, out of nothing, and it is meaning which thrills him: he is in the crucible of meaning. Every contact, for the lover, raises the question of an answer: the skin is asked to reply."

This predicament, though, is one of immense danger. In the "Uncertainty of Signs" chapter of *A Lover's Discourse* Barthes writes:

> "A man who wants the truth is never answered save in strong, highly colored images, which nonetheless turn ambiguous, indecisive, once he tries to transform them into signs: as in any manticism, the consulting lover must make his own truth...Signs are not proofs, since anyone can produce false or ambiguous signs."

*

Telling Larissa about M took the entirety of one of our sessions and without comment from her I talked the whole time, going into great detail on the serendipity of our meeting and how close I felt to M even though we'd just begun dating. The sex, yes, and that I was no longer unwillingly celibate, yes. But none of that mattered at all. No, I *liked* M. And she *liked* me. Near and far, I could already see our intertangled futures in the distance. When I was forced to tell Larissa that it'd only been three weeks since our reintroduction I felt bad that she had to ask, that a person—a therapist—could be so clueless as to what, even in all my considered cynicism, I couldn't help but classify as crystallizing new love. The amount of time we'd been together didn't matter nearly as much as the feelings between us did.

*

And yet.

*

"What I have called crystallization is a mental process which draws from everything that happens new proofs of the perfection of the loved one" writes Stendhal in *On Love*.

Proof of perfection as rendered in strong, highly colored images that waver indecisively. Only the lover, that most assured and unreliable of narrators, can perceive his own truth, however fictional it might be. Limerent, I carried a vision of M with me everywhere I went while we were seeing one another. In its inconstancy this vision proved remarkably consistent.

*

When at my insistence M and I asked each other the thirty-six "closeness-generating procedure" questions outlined in Arthur Aron's paper "The Experimental Generation of Interpersonal Closeness"—I'd already printed out and asked her to read Mandy Len Catron's "To Fall in Love With Anyone, Do This" essay based on the formulations made in "The Experimental Generation..."—we both shared the exact same answer to questions 16 and 35: *What do you value most in a friendship?* and *Of all the people in your family, whose death would you find most disturbing?* and *16. What do you value most in a friendship?* We also shared very similar answers to *3. Before making a telephone call, do you ever rehearse what you are going to say? Why?* and *24. How do you feel about your relationship with your mother?*

Lying alone that night in bed, unable to sleep, I couldn't help but imagine and imagine. Technicolor, Surround-Sound, rife with stereotype and cliché, it felt like the first time I'd ever done so.

*

M.

*

XXIX. A man who is vexed by too much passion usually does not love.

*

When my long verbal onslaught was concluded at the initial therapy session where I told Larissa about M, I asked her what she thought. Rarely at a loss for words, this time Larissa paused for what felt like a minor eternity. *Well, I think that our real work in here can now begin* she finally said, flashing a small smile. I smiled back. *That sounds exactly like something that a therapist would say.* We kept smiling. *What did you expect?* she said, her face a newly painted wall, still damp with wet paint.

*

Two and a half months later I stopped seeing Larissa.

*

A month after that, after we'd been dating for five months, M broke up with me via text while she was working a flight out of town. She was going to move to New York after all. Or maybe Cologne. But let's stay in touch, for sure, and wasn't it great that we were able to link up for a bit after all that?! She was super glad that I'd been there for her. And the Bauer show that I'd helped everyone with had turned out amazing!

*

The mind plays tricks on itself in a game the body keeps forgetting the rules to, idealized outcomes far realer than ones stark-bright right in front. Product of our imagination, daimons aren't real but the thoughts and actions they invigorate in us last far longer than we might like to believe.

*

Roland Barthes' solitude is a largely impersonal one. "The lover's solitude is not a solitude of person (love confides, speaks, tells itself), it is a solitude of system: I am alone in making a system out of it (perhaps because I am ceaselessly flung back on the solipsism of my discourse)" being the way he puts it in *A Lover's Discourse.* Constantly recurring, that notion: systemic, the systematic solipsism of one's discourse, my discourse. It's mine alone but it's filled with everything and everyone else inside of it, particularly those I love or think I love or hope to love or—

*

"Instead of leaving the box, I shall enclose the world within it" imparts Kobo Abe's box man. Who's to say which is which though? Boxy, the world is as flat as one makes it. Immobile and unchanging, what's allowed in can, if one so chooses, be only what's allowed out.

*

In my second to last meeting with Larissa, before I impulsively decided to stop seeing her, she asked me a simple question. At that point I'd been her patient for ten and ½ months. Having finished my graduate coursework, defended my doctoral dissertation and nearly finished teaching my classes at MU, I was moving back to the West Coast in half a year, maybe less. I still had time, but it was lessening in steady rivulets.

I'd been discussing *The Gambler* and "The Kreutzer Sonata," how even though the protagonists were different in multiple ways the endings of both works came to pass in a similar manner, with Tolstoy's Pozdnyshev and Dostoevsky's Alexei finding hope in their ability to persevere through suffering. It was truly admirable, I said, to believe in something that is not true, that will never be true. Earlier I'd been telling Larissa how happy I was dating M, even though such a statement was, at best, a half-truth. Really I was scared, nervous and fearful. Like Pozdnyshev and Alexei I'd somehow activated in my mind the notion that I had a pronounced taste for self-pity and loss, and it was these contentions of mine that, in relating to Larissa how much I enjoyed M's company, how good things seemed to be going for me all of a sudden, I was hoping to refute out loud.

She was staring at me. *When does it stop?* I'd been talking without concern for whether Larissa was listening, unaware that my voice was the only one that had been heard all session. *Does what stop?* I said. Looking tired, she glowered, seeming to have to strain not to point accusingly at me. *All of this co-opting of other people's—fictional people, dead people— pain and suffering under the guise of making yourself feel better.* Befuddled, I gawked at her blankly. *I like to read and to think about* I started to say but Larissa cut me off with a wave of her hand. *Look, I know what you're doing. That's why I'm here.* I was starting to hate her all over again. *What am I doing then?* I asked, my irritation evident, written in big block Sharpie marker all over my face. *What you're doing is trying to hide that you might be wrong.* A steamy greenhouse of shivs and daggers, I glared. *Wrong about what?* Larissa got up from the couch, her body full and heavy as it made its way across the room to her desk, late morning sun splashing at regular intervals as she walked. She opened a drawer and got out a granola bar. It'd been almost an hour and our session was nearly over. *Well, you're right* she said. *Maybe wrong isn't the right word. But listening to you talk today I can't help but think that you're trying too hard.* Still I glared. *Trying too hard at what?* Again she gave a slight wave of her hand. *At all of it. All of it without the overthinking and self-interpreting and sabotaging and all of it. At just coming to terms with the only version of your self you'll ever have, no matter the place or situation or*...She trailed off, glancing out the window and averting eye contact.

Smirking, I stood up, facing Larissa directly. I was only too happy not to have to deal with this shit for a while. *I thought you didn't really like Freud* I said. *Because that for sure sounds meaningless and Freudian. To the core.* I was spouting nonsense—what she had said sounded nothing like Freud and I knew it—but I didn't care. I wanted to make clear to her that she sucked at her job. I was already planning how to cancel my next appointment in as unassuming a way as possible. But firmly unassuming, in a manner that yet sent a message of assumption. *Oh, it doesn't have much to do with Freud.* Larissa briefly paused. *It has to do with being able to see your self for who you are without having to rely on anyone else, no Tolstoy or Dostoevsky or the imagination. Or M or R or L or even people like me.* I was still facing her, ready to turn my back and walk out. *Are you seriously telling me to stop reading? Or to stop trying to be happy?* Larissa shook her head. *No, I'm just asking you to come to some form of acceptance about who you are.* I kept staring at her. *I expected something more enigmatic* I said. But she was biting into the granola bar, chewing, her mouth full. *Have a good week* she said after swallowing, benignly ushering me out. *I'll see you next week.*

*

From the diaries of Cesare Pavese—5th October, 1938:

You cannot insult a man more atrociously than by refusing to believe he is suffering.

*

From the diaries of Cesare Pavese—15th October, 1938:

To accept suffering (Dostoevsky) is, in essence, a way of not suffering...But Dostoevsky's theory is that one ceases to suffer only by accepting it. And it seems that one can accept suffering only by sacrificing oneself...One accepts suffering (resignation), and then realizes that all there is to it is that one has suffered. It has done us no good... So we grit our teeth and grow cynical. The thing that always hurts us most is to feel we have been fooled, to see our suffering denied, rendered of no account.

*

Entails equating suffering with self-worth, one of my own definitions of prudery. To see and to want and to not take, then chastising oneself for wanting in the first place. Suffering as a means of release, encircling the self in a vacating that seems to just keep going and going, relentless.

*

Being that she was a former patient of Larissa's, I called my friend K and, receiving no response, texted her. *I think I'm going to stop seeing Larissa. Just don't think it's going anywhere now. Thoughts?* K texted back a few short minutes later, writing *Interesting. I was just contemplating making an appt. to go to back to see her.* I studied that sentence on my phone. *Why? What's up?* I responded. K didn't get back to me until the next day. *Because out of the four therapists I've seen in my life, she was the one that helped me the most. She actually made me think super painfully hard and that made me think about changing. Or trying to change.*

I didn't care. I wasn't going back.

*

After I stopped seeing Larissa and M stopped seeing me—she hadn't left town yet but soon, to Seattle now or probably Chicago—I stayed in Missouri for another four and a half months, one full academic semester. During that time I casually dated around town, sleeping with two women and attempting to sleep with more. What did it matter? I was leaving soon and knew it, told anyone who asked or didn't that I wasn't going to be in town for much longer. Past was past; I wouldn't contain myself in it any longer. Believing this, I thought, gave me a certain kind of power, along with an inability to get hurt. I began to drink heavily three to four nights a week, attempting to hit on any woman at the bar who offhand-glanced my way. Although common for some men in their twenties and thirties (and forties and fifties and...), this was completely out of character for me. But to believe oneself terminally unique is to unbelieve the seven and a half billion other people on the planet, each with their own afflictions, syndromes, problems and quirks. What difference did it make anyway? Who cared? Mortal, everyone is terminal. But no one is unique, especially my own endlessly unique self. Drunkenly I was anybody else and that was the point. In my head I was already gone.

*

"I'm grossed out about sex being used as a tool for power, about people not giving a shit about who they're putting their dick into... I've known a lot of people that have been heavily damaged by some asshole's drunken hard-on" imparts Jeff Mangum, discussing Neutral Milk Hotel's "Song against Sex."

*

And yet.

*

A distinct childhood memory of mine: junior year of high school attending my first formal dance with L, a girl I had no romantic interest in but one that I'd asked to go with me because she was close friends with all the girls that my friends were going with. (Youth.) While at dinner L and I had nothing to talk about and shared zero chemistry; she was either shy, uninterested or both of those things and in my ill-fitting suit, clammy hands and scrubbed clean forehead, I behaved the exact same way.

After dinner's tedium we made it to the dance and I lost L for a bit, which was a relief. I hung on the sidelines with my friends, talking about what we were going to do afterwards and how lame this thing really was. I mean, I definitely thought it was going to be lame, but not this lame. Stupid lame. This is *so* lame. Can you believe how—

A few tables down, then, I spied L talking to a group of people I knew but wasn't very friendly with. I was a skater and the people L stood laughing with were somewhere between *organized-athlete* clique and *let's-go-drinking-and-motocrossing-up-in-the-hills* clique. We co-existed without issue, but I went to a relatively big high school—my graduating class had 650+ students—and different social groups were, of course, omnipresent. Prior to asking her to the dance I didn't know if L was dating someone else and I hadn't cared to talk with her to find out.

Watching her from a distance, though, I suddenly got the urge to ask L to dance, to make out with her, to elucidate to anyone in attendance that *I'd* asked L to go with me to this thing, that even if we weren't dating we were on a date tonight. Undulating fierce inside of me, this was a strange sensation that I'd never felt before, but I didn't try to question or shake it. Instead I acted, in a fever.

Although she seemed surprised when I asked, L danced with me and then later, on a torn loveseat in a dimly lit attic at a house party near our high school, kissed me for a half-hearted minute before she abruptly got up and left the room, leaving me alone. We'd barely talked the whole night and I still felt no romantic emotion, but I surprisingly found myself angry at her. Angry for saying yes to my invitation to the dance even though we didn't know one and other and didn't want to know one and other; angry that for nearly the entirety of the evening we'd appeared as two separate and distinct entities rather than as one unified, enjoying-themselves-together whole. Irate that she'd just left the room and, buzzed, now it was left to me to figure out whose house I was at and how I was going to get home. I'd never felt it before that night, this rage, and it would be too simplistic to say it derived from some sense of rejection or betrayal I inexplicably felt at L's hands. Directed at my own real or perceived inadequacies, the anger came out of nowhere or nowhere I could place at that young point in my life. Formal dance night junior year of high school was the first time it surfaced but, even in my shy and oft-prudish ways, it wouldn't be the last time.

*

"Every woman's a whore. / I can't communicate" intones a disembodied male voice in Sylvia Plath's poem "Lesbos." Well-known but not one of the poet's universally acclaimed works, "Lesbos" relates the anger the poem's speaker (a stand-in for Plath herself) feels for a dysfunctionally married couple that seem to subconsciously take pleasure in that dysfunction. "O vase of acid, / It is love you are full of. You know who you hate…Every day you fill him with soul-stuff, like a pitcher. / You are exhausted." Although not entirely taken with the woman in the relationship either, Plath nevertheless feels solidarity with the way she feels forced to build up her husband's confidence, day in, day out. It's exhausting to do so for the wife—and yet wholly required, expected, necessary. For this act of selflessness, though, all she receives in return is a dull silence. "I can't communicate" and that's that, the end of it. Let's not talk, can we. Let's sit. Let's just sit.

*

"…as I hate sex,
the man's mouth
sealing my mouth, the man's
paralyzing body—"

In Louise Glück's poem "Mock Orange" it's a sexual expectation that's reviled whereas in Plath's "Lesbos" it's an emotional one, the kind that, paradoxically subdued and aggressive, is apt to drain any partner or significant other.

*

In his February 24, 2018 *New York Times* opinion piece "Real Men Get Rejected, Too" Moises Velasquez-Manoff writes that at an early age boys often learn to wear full-bodied masks that unfortunately mold into who and how they are as men. The "shame-hardening process" that occurs for many adolescent males in Western culture turns into a relishing of sexual power that defines their whole scope of masculinity. Velasquez-Manoff states, "Most men are not, I'd wager, serial harassers or rapists. But problematic male behavior seems widespread enough that it suggests our conception of masculinity is flawed." He goes on to assert that for certain men "it is precisely the power imbalance that's erotic," whereas others overconform to "common, if exaggerated, notions of masculinity. [These men are] doing a five-star rendition of what they think manhood requires."

As a father, Velasquez-Manoff recommends talking to one's children early about what it means to be a man, elucidating for them that manliness does not come in one stereotypical and/or sexist swath or type. Emphasizing that romantic rejection is a (needed) part of life is equally important, as is discussing sex and sexuality with one's kids generally. (If silence is golden it's a fool's gold, shiny on the outside and empty within.) Praising the quote unquote "feminine" aspects of masculinity that certain men strain to bury or hide, Velasquez-Manoff ends "Real Men Get Rejected, Too" by declaring that "many men's need for self-aggrandizement, for confirmation about our prowess — what [psychologist Richard Weissbourd] called the "narcissism of male desire" — shows just how fragile the construct of manhood can be… It produces brittle people in constant need of shoring up."

*

"The problem of woman is the most marvelous and disturbing problem in all the world" decreed André Breton in 1929. Then and now that may be so. The problem of man is a much simpler one. It is the problem of a humanness that needs to seek to change. It is the problem of a humanness that needs to change.

*

When I was younger talking to my father about masculinity and its fallacies would have been anathema; I wouldn't have listened if he tried. (Which I'm sure he did. I was trying hard not to pay attention.) I bumbled my way into things the way most of my male peers did, two steps forward, one step back. The man I became, then, changed from day to day. Certainly I needed shoring up more often than I would have liked to admit, but I also resisted—or so I told my self—the trappings of boorish maleness. Even in my mid-twenties when I was sleeping around with whomever whenever, I still liked to believe that I was behaving in a way that mirrored my female partners, where desire was mutual, consent voiced, and relationship statuses or lack thereof made manifest. A preying pickup artist I was not.

Drunk those final fours months in Missouri, though, I became who I never thought I'd be, perched lecherously on my barstool. "Every woman's a whore" and only by believing that can the shaky scenario otherwise known as the male self be somehow made to feel whole, full of "soul-stuff." Even bashful, self-conscious men like me, I learned, can turn into wanton pricks with the help of alcohol's false confidence and insecurity's deep pockets.

*

That asshole, I brought books to the bar regularly. Collections of poetry or books of critical theory, nonfiction. Plutarch's *Lives* one night and a biography of the musician Cat Power the next. *Vanishing Point* by David Markson or *Siste Viator* by Sarah Manguso. I wouldn't read them intently or sometimes at all. Each was instead a security blanket, a way of telling my lonely self that, even if I was drunk at the bar alone, I could at any time tune out and immerse myself in a different reality, different mask. Some people constantly check their phones. I bring sweaty paperbacks.

It's a paradox of my life as a reader that the books that have been most important to me I've never been able to finish. *Tristram Shandy. The Cantos. The Waves. The Pillow Book. Juneteenth. Don Quixote.* Some short, others long. A few I had problems completing due to my incomprehension, but more often I didn't want the experience to be over because I enjoyed the book to such a degree. These books are still works in progress, marked as FINISH *Don Quixote* or FINISH *The Waves* on my To-Do list. For years they've been listed as such. Having peeked, I know how each volume ends, and I know how that end is arrived at. It's the prolongment of conclusion, though, that I savor, an ongoingness that allows me to exist in the book without its ever being finished. This quirk of mine, I'm sure, has some deep-rooted psychological reason for its embedment in me. *You're treading sand, you're trying to drown on land* Larissa might say, displaying her elliptical half-smile. I don't doubt it.

Another of these never-to-be-completed books is Michel Leiris's *Manhood: A Journey from Childhood into the Fierce Order of Virility* and it's what I began bringing to the bar the last weeks of my living in Missouri. Although I'd started reading it at least three times prior, this time I became absorbed in an entirely new way. After a few nights of trying to read, drink and leer at women at the same time, I cut out the leering and most of the drinking and eventually, in the final month of my Midwestern existence, stopped going to the bar entirely. I studied Leiris's *Manhood* at my house instead, painstakingly trying not to finish it.

Originally published in France in 1939 and translated into English in 1963,

Manhood is a strange tome and one that I feel no small amount of envy towards for a simple reason: in it Leiris writes my autobiography 60+ years before my birth. (All great works of literature do this, of course; by telling their stories they dawn light on our own. If we're lucky, though, we don't realize this fact.) In her 1964 foreword to Leiris's book Susan Sontag writes that "*Manhood* is an exercise in shamelessness—a sequence of self-exposures of a craven, morbid, damaged temperament...Leiris must feel, as he writes, the equivalent of the bullfighter's knowledge that he risks being gored. Only then is writing worthwhile." Believing that, in his unwillingness to display standard and perfunctory masculine traits and behaviors, Leiris ultimately exists to "appall" his readers, Sontag opines that "...the greatest problem Leiris faces is the chronic thinness of his emotions... his failure ever to be at home in his own body." What others might see as a lack, though, Sontag views positively, finding worth in the way *Manhood* "violates many [literary] preconceptions." That the book is often boring as well— according to Sontag it has "no movement or direction and provides no consummation or climax"—serves its own purpose. Full of routine and rigidity, most people's lives are extremely boring, and if we are to accept *Manhood* as "part of the project of a life" it should behave accordingly. So it does and in Sontag's eyes it is worth lauding because of this.

*

Leiris is clinical in his self-examination, to the point that what might normally be called the self is left naked, alone and destitute on *Manhood*'s cutting room floor. Far from being just a clever bit of Rimbaudian wordplay, I is truly an Other in Leiris's view, and should be treated as such.

*

Years earlier L had first introduced me to *Manhood,* giving it to me as a pseudo-anniversary gift ("This is not an anniversary gift" she'd written on the bookmark enclosed within) after we'd been dating for 6 months. Taking the book as some type of veiled code or question, I wasn't sure what to think, and I flitted through it at random for a few confusing weeks. Next to a sentence reading "It has been some time, in any case, since I have ceased to consider the sexual act as a simple matter, but rather as a relatively exceptional act, necessitating certain inner accommodations that are either particularly tragic or particularly exalted, but very different, in either case, from what I regard as my usual disposition" I'd written in a now-faded red ink the statement-posing-as-a-question "His usual disposition is abnormal but unknown to us and him."

Beyond that jotting, though, no record exists of my having thumbed through *Manhood* when L originally gifted it to me, and my memories of initially skimming through are equally hazy. At the age of 25 I hadn't known what to make of Leiris's text, had wondered why L had bestowed the book upon me—why *Manhood* and why then, six months into our relationship? I wondered and wondered but refused to ask L or actually read Leiris's book, which, just in flitting, I found to be confusingly insular and allusive. I put it aside and instead jealously watched L onstage, singing right at me and everyone else.

*

Even though I didn't plan on reading it anytime soon, I kept *Manhood*, taking it with me as I moved from place to place. Acutely stoned one night soon after landing in Bellingham, my books only recently having found their place on the shelves again, I remember staring at the cover of Leiris's book in fascinated disgust. Featuring an illustration of German Renaissance painter Lucas Cranach the Elder's work "Lucretia and Judith" (an archetypal image that figures prominently in Leiris's life) that finds on the left panel a naked Lucretia somewhat passively stabbing herself between the breasts and on the right a naked Judith holding the decapitated head of the general Holofernes (a war chief contemporary of Nebuchadnezzar II, the King of Babylon from 605 BC-562 BC) in her lowered left hand, her eyes blissed-out, it's an alarming sight to behold, this cover. Black and white itself, Cranach the Elder's painting is bordered and overlaid by a middling barf brown hue, which also serves as the color of the book's spine and front/back cover. To my eyes it's one of the ugliest book covers ever conceived and that stoned night early into my first Bellingham sojourn I studied *Manhood*'s outer shell in mild revulsion. Glancing inside, all I found were letters upon words upon long sentences and paragraphs, each of which seemed to go further away from what I was looking for as an aspiringly virile man. What I wanted couldn't be found in a book, I thought, and certainly not this one. I stuck *Manhood* back on the shelf and, new in town, resolved to go looking for my own conception of the abstraction that Leiris had chosen for his book title.

*

From the diaries of Cesare Pavese—3rd April, 1939:

Every man has the philosophy of his own aptitudes.

And what that man's aptitudes are, then, determine how his philosophy will help or hinder him, loudly sound his passions or meekly silence them.

That word, philosophy. How I revile its smugness.

*

And yet.

*

Years later I rediscovered *Manhood* before moving across the country again, back to Bellingham once more, and this time I finally recognized Leiris's text for the affirmation that it is. Such a belief of mine is at odds with Sontag's vision of the author—who in her "Foreword" writes of Leiris's "loathing" for himself, "recording the defeats of his own virility; completely incompetent in the arts of the body…"—and to a certain degree Leiris's himself. To use just one example from many, midway through *Manhood* Leiris states:

"If it is a beautiful day, I am filled with anxiety: it's a bad sign that the weather should be so fine, what terrible event is in store? Similarly, if I take any pleasure at all, I calculate my chances of paying for it in the near future, and a hundred times over! for fate is nothing but a usurer."

This, then, is Leiris in a relatively sanguine, glass half-full moment. If it can't get any darker than that it does.

*

What does it mean to be a man? What makes him? Questions like these are normally answered with a small slew of platitudes, none of which warrant acknowledgment here. For Leiris, though, manhood can be characterized as the harnessing of a stern objectivity in the face of a world-wide humanness that by default revels in all manners of perverse subjectivity and self-involvement. Leiris would identify with Phillip Lopate's contention in his essay "Against Joie de Vivre" that "[t]o know rapture is to have one's whole life poisoned." Unlike Lopate, however, Leiris is not searching for anything—there is no solution or antidote— and *Manhood* is not a book that purports itself to be hungry for satisfaction of any kind. Instead it is dedicated to the thorough accepting of one's *wrongness*, and with this acceptance comes a severe personal risk that, for Leiris, literally means the difference between life and death.

As Sontag mentions in her Foreword to the book, the trope that Leiris uses here is that of the bullfighter. In the same way that a bullfighter's every movement in the ring is authentic, either staying or inducing death, the truly confessional writer is so "severe" with himself as to be, for certain readers no doubt, inappropriately intimate; however untoward or shameful, nothing of consequence can be left out. Disregarding the opinions and feelings of friends and loved ones, transgressing prevailing societal norms and decorums, even, by din of one's confession, allowing for the possibility of physical harm or jail time—such is the burden of truth that an authentic writer of confessions must bear.

But, as Leiris relates in *Manhood's* Afterword, that is only a beginning:

> "For to the tell the whole truth and nothing but the truth is not all: [the writer] must also confront it directly and tell it without artifice, without those great arias intended to make it acceptable, tremolos or catches in the voice, grace notes and gildings which would have no other result than to disguise it to whatever degree, even by merely attenuating its crudity, by making less noticeable what might be shocking about it."

Certainly there are established codes and rules the bullfighter must adhere to while in the ring, but the most important one—separating once-in-a-lifetime bullfighters from exceptional ones, exceptional ones from the merely memorable, etc.—involves the degree of deathly exposure they are willing to expose themselves to. Dance around with the bull and the audience is entertained; become the bull, as one, and the audience is forever changed. Such was Leiris's guide in writing *Manhood*. Mere exposure is never enough. Great acts of life and art demand and deserve more.

*

In his essay "Benefit of Clergy: Some Notes on Salvador Dali" George Orwell writes:

"Autobiography is only to be trusted when it reveals something disgraceful. A man who gives a good account of himself is probably lying, since any life when viewed from the inside is simply a series of defeats."

Although Leiris would take issue with Orwell's use of the word disgraceful here (being that, if nothing else, what is disgraceful is always and irrevocably *true*), these contentions of Orwell's would otherwise find favor with the author of *Manhood.* To be a man is to live inside a series of defeats, and the best men simply accept this fact as soon as they come of age. Transgressing, this allows them the freedom to succeed.

*

What I immediately identified with (and still identify with) in *Manhood* is Leiris's prudish tendencies that belie a greater sense of passion and passionate sensitivity. When Leiris is on the verge of losing his virginity— "the dreamed-of moment"— his "excitement was so great that [he] proved incapable of the least demonstration of virility" and a second appointment with his lover must be made; he is too stimulated to maintain an erection. (In the first weeks of my dating L a similar thing happened to me, although after a few minutes of unsteadiness I was able to persevere.) Both willingly and unwillingly celibate for parts of the book, Leiris suddenly goes "cold and silent" while out on dates with women he is supremely interested in, instilling confusion in both parties. In his dealings with the opposite sex he is fearful and timorous—but completely enraptured. Although he can objectively describe his feelings, motivations and actions, Leiris is a contradiction of subjective selfhood in *Manhood.* He possesses a withering vein of suicidal ideation in the book yet does not die (born in 1901, he lived until 1990, perishing at the age of eighty-nine), instead choosing to constantly spear at the little tendrils of life everywhere around him. Leiris cannot consider love "save as a kind of failure" but, in love, gets and stays married. As noted, he prizes objectivity and authenticity above all else. That said, he takes a "certain sensual pleasure in the manipulation of language" in his youth, devoting himself to studying Surrealism and writing poetry, both activities which profoundly informed his later objectively rendered confessional autobiographies.

To be sure, Sontag is right in that the many debasements and abjections that occur in *Manhood* cannot be viewed positively by anyone with a reasonable grasp on reality. Leiris himself is unbendingly critical of his younger self's actions but, looking back in the volume's Prologue, he nevertheless calls his youth "the only happy period of my life."

*

"I can see which is the better course to take, and I agree with it; but I follow the worse" is how one translation of Ovid's puts it. As Leiris elucidates throughout *Manhood*, though, the mark of a fully realized man is accepting this worseness and navigating its contours fully and unashamedly, without self-censure. Unlike Sontag, I don't think Leiris possesses any particularly trenchant form of self-loathing. Nor do I think that his emotions are chronically thin, or that the book only exists to appall his more "normal" and normalized readers.

On the contrary, reading ¾'s of *Manhood* (I know how it ends but don't tell me) that last month in Missouri I finally understood that distinctions such as better or worse mean comparatively little within the context of the trash heap that stereotypical masculinity so often seems to be. Acted out in only one way, within only one framework, manhood is a sham that, masking, veils far more than it enlightens. In writing his own unvarnished and unrelenting book on the subject Leiris (knowingly or not) places great value in his traditionally unmanly errors, failures and miscalculations, thereby showing the reader how, even when they're deeply engrained in culture and society, mirages like masculinity are just that.

*

Focused on coming to terms with his own personal identity and sense of self before attempting to understand anyone else's, Leiris is a 20th century Millennial, existing one hundred years before that generational term came into vogue. At all costs Leiris's desire for individual understanding overrides sexual desires or societal compatibility, and even if he doesn't wholly comprehend who or how he is by *Manhood*'s end it's the uncompromising candor of Leiris's pursuit that I find admirable. Attempting to fully understand himself before forcing other people to try and do so partially, what Sontag found appalling, if alluringly so, simply allures me. In its inappropriateness Leiris's intimacy with the reader is made complete—and unforgettable.

*

The school year over and my long ten-year-run as a student in higher education finally completed, I found myself living in Bellingham for the second time, overeducated and very alone. Settling in, I took a much-needed break from drinking, moved into a quiet one-bedroom apartment in the city's Southeast quadrant. I could throw a rock and hit my local coffee shop and dog park; I was refreshed and intent on creative and professional productivity. With an established small press I published my first collection of poems and, although thrilling, what personal or artistic solution that might have provided me initially didn't eventually. Months passed. I made new friends and reconnected with old ones, adjuncted as an English instructor at colleges close to my apartment and far away. Even with the heavy rain and the higher prices and the longer lines, I enjoyed living in the Pacific Northwest again. It was home.

Although there were far more women with likeminded interests and inclinations for me to date in Bellingham as compared to Columbia, I largely abstained from trying to do so, telling my self that I needn't rush anything and that I didn't want to sully the burgeoning cluster of friends I was making by dating within my social group. I showed up but by choice stayed on the outside of the circle, peering in with great interest and curiosity. I evinced no forward movement, though. For now, peering would alone suffice.

Nine months into my living back in Washington, then, I came to the immediate conclusion that nearly all my life had been lived insufferably seriously, self-involved and nose-thick in books. Walking by a local comedy club one afternoon I, on a whim, enrolled in an eight-week improv comedy class. And then another. And another. Although I was always just an enthusiastic dilettante, what improv forced me to do was live in a moment that was rarely of my own creation; I never knew what my scene partner(s) was going to say or do and that freedom enabled me to forget the possibility, focus on the actual. To great laughs from the audience I occasionally acted out my prudish tendencies onstage, lightly pawing at my fellow scene mates while they tried to figure out what I wanted. It was in the contrast and contradiction between our words and movements that laughter arrived, with my invested aloofness baffling and titillating my scene partners' straight-man normality. Life imitates art; art imitates life.

*

The contrast between thought and action, intent and actuality. And the contradictory state the most human one, always. Writing about *The Talented Mr. Ripley* author Patricia Highsmith in *The New York Times Style Magazine* in 2021, Rennie McDougall contends that Highsmith's work "revealed the writer as she was, a multitude of warring selves—the public and the private, the moral and the degenerate, the loving and the conniving." It's a war impossible to win, selfhood, with each human being an aggregation of different parts, contexts and contours. Yet on we fight. If, as the queer theorist Gloria E. Anzaldúa asserted, "[i]dentity is a river—a process" and that one's self "needs to flow, to change to stay a river," then surely the waters alternately rage and wane over the course of a single day, let alone a whole lifetime. The only constant is the unknowing, the unexpected, the unforeseen.

*

"Each self begins with a rift and a revelation" decrees E.M. Cioran in his book *The Trouble With Being Born* (1973). A revelatory rift and no transformation or revolution is possible without first undergoing the proper scissions.

*

Or, as in the Buddhist tradition, studying the self to displace it. Whole life long, studying to forget.

And then all the nothing else.

*

Time passed. I adulted as best I could. And from the outside this pose no doubt appeared successful. The question of wrongness, though, lingered. *What you're doing is trying to hide that you might be wrong* Larissa had told me and still I didn't know what that meant. Was I wrong in reading rather than living? In placing too much faith in my self while not really knowing which self of mine would ever show up? In not being direct with others about my desires? In being too sentimental and sensitive? In hiding out in school rather than attempting to face the "real" world head-on? Was it that I spent too much time stewing in the past rather than carpe dieming the future? In not finding a partner and lying to my self about why that hadn't happened? All of those things? Some of them— or none at all?

Suddenly I was thirty-two, then thirty-three, and watched as friends old and new—all Millennials who had, in their twenties, denigrated the institution of marriage, deeming it outdated and unnecessary, definitely not for them—got married. Whether they'd slept around widely in their youth or not at all, these friends had now found where their selfhood existed in deep connection with someone else's, and from the edge of the circle at each wedding I ate cake and sipped soda water, cheering as I watched the transformation take place under the societal-sanctioned eyes of the state. I was happy for them all and went home alone.

*

And yet.

*

Writing about the playwright Young Jean Lee's work in *The New York Times Magazine*, specifically her play "Straight White Men," critic Parul Sehgal states, "Lee's work is about wrongness: about being the wrong kind of man, woman, Asian; about saying the wrong thing; about getting other people wrong. Her characters are ill at ease in their bodies and in the world…" Sehgal goes on to state that in "Straight White Men" Lee "drills into something more core. Shuck off, subvert, cleave to your gender or race all you like, but a universal horror of weakness remains—a collective orientation toward status, power, control."

*

One of my own definitions of prudery entails feeling one's sexuality is wrong in some very defined and vague way and not knowing where or how rightness might be enacted.

*

"There are people who give themselves over to their sexuality, there are people who lose themselves in it, but, for me, sex is something very painful, very melancholy, because one sees oneself" imparts French author Leïla Slimani in a 2018 feature on her and her work. For Slimani and her characters desire can be so far-reaching that it obliterates all else; seeing one's true sexual self is shameful, something deeply felt and still unknowable.

*

"But I guess I just feel like that is sort of what the message has been to me, or how I've interpreted messages: that my sexuality is actually really dangerous and disgusting" imparts novelist Ottessa Moshfegh in a 2018 feature on her and her work. Unlike Slimani, though, for Moshfegh this dangerous disgust is less sad than comical. A thing to fight against, then accept, then flaunt wide-open for all to see. The more *twisted* one is the more they matter. The more they circumvent the senseless sleepy strictures that culture boxes everyone in with, especially in terms of gender and sexuality, the likelier it is that they have something worthwhile to say or do.

*

In Young Jean Lee's "Straight White Men" it's the character of Matt who's wrong. Although he's educated, capable, diligent, and (seemingly) willing, something holds him back from success. (Or so believe his successful father and two successful brothers.) What holds him back is himself. Contemplating what his dead mother might have said about his situation, Matt states towards the end the play: "She would say there's nothing you can do to erase the problems of your own existence. She would tell me not to despair, and to keep trying to find my way." But this way of Matt's differs from the normal one that success often finds itself at. "Straight White Men" ends with Matt sitting alone, looking blankly out at the audience, confused and forsaken.

*

In Lee's play "Pullman, WA" the character of Pete expresses the same sentiment as Matt in a different way, asserting:

> "For me, I have never felt like I was me. There was always something wrong with who I was so that I was always thinking of myself as some future-existing person, someone who—like an outline of someone—oh shit, it's hard to talk about this stuff.
>
> "Okay. There is this idea that some people have that they don't count if they are fucked-up in some way.
>
> "Like this idea of being fat. If you're fat, then you're not who you're supposed to be. You're supposed to be thin. So when you're fat, it's like you don't count, like you're not you. Does that make sense?"

*

A distinct childhood memory of mine: watching my close friend A try and learn how to ollie on his skateboard in between sixth and seventh grade. In the back of Bailey's Restaurant on Skyline Boulevard, the hottest summer ever. Over and over again A riding full blast into the dead grass and just before doing so lifting the tail of his board, quickly sliding his left foot over the griptape from back to front, attempting to lift off into the air. But he couldn't do it and we'd been sweating there for hours. Having already been skateboarding for several months, my friends and I gave him pointers and kept demonstrating for him, easy as pie, but it just didn't work; he couldn't get it. He couldn't. Eventually we wordlessly decided that today was not going to be the day and, after leaving A with encouraging words, we all skated home, grateful to not have to watch such dedicated suffering anymore. Even if they wish they did, some people just don't have it. When I left A was still there, panting, determined. It was a sad sight to see.

*

"You're not who you're supposed to be."

*

Six months later A was by far the best skateboarder in our group. He skated every day, making it a central part of his young life. By the time we were in high school he was sponsored by a local skateshop and after high school he moved to Southern California to be a part of the skateboard industry. For a number of years, he was a professional skateboarder.

*

"You're not who you're supposed to be."

*

For years my cousin F works as the assistant manager at a small, perennially underachieving independent movie theater. And then one morning she wakes up and starts studying for the LSAT. Thirty-four years old. Six months later she takes the test, receives an overwhelmingly high score, is eventually offered full ride scholarships at Georgetown and Stanford and Brown. Choosing Georgetown, she graduates at the head of her class and now works as a public defender in Washington D.C., an impossible job that she is impossibly good at.

*

Born in a town of 13,000 residents in rural Northwestern Nevada, my friend R grows up frightened of his desires. He wants to be mastered, is interested in bondage and submission and discipline and edgeplay. He also likes men. Never to be spoken or even thought about, either of those things. Upon graduating from high school R moves to an even smaller town in New Hampshire, where he assumes he will stew alone in his want to a greater degree. For months this proves to be the case, until one night R begins anonymously talking online to a man who, it's eventually revealed, lives near him and shares his sexual and social interests. They meet; they test the waters. R has never allowed himself any of this. That initial man proves to be a non-starter for R, but it doesn't matter—he has always known who he is privately, but doing so publicly changes everything for R. He starts to search out what before he silenced. Everywhere he goes now he values why and how he is. He thrives.

*

"You're not who you're supposed to be—" and it doesn't matter. It isn't and wasn't true.

*

"The truth about who you are lies not at the root of the tree but rather out at the tips of the branches, the thousand tips" writes Lewis Hyde in his book *A Primer for Forgetting: Getting Past the Past.*

*

The thousand tips. The hundreds of thousands of thousands of tips.

*

"Every man is not only himself. Men are lived over again" imparts Sir Thomas Browne in *Religio Medici*, his 17th century volume of psychological inquiry. Who we once were is not who we are and, product of the imagination, our daimons change accordingly, day by day, year by year. Although it can feel good in the moment, boxing oneself into any fixed identity or mentality is a fool's errand, doomed to stagnation and, ultimately, failure.

*

Entails finally embracing the moment and forgetting all else, one of my own definitions of prudery. To forget and in doing so finding. And accepting.

*

Today it is Thursday the twenty-second. Skyping with Larissa yesterday— something that I now do three times a month once again— I told her that I can't help but believe that L was the only woman I've ever truly loved, eternal, and that believing this scares me to no small degree. ("We love only once, for only are we perfectly equipped for loving…And on how that first true love-affair shapes itself depends the pattern of our lives" writes Cyril Connolly in *The Unquiet Grave.*) *She was the one that got away* I say and Larissa half-smiles at my use of the cliché, doesn't respond for a long second. And then says *That's entirely normal, I think, although remember that the way you think about her now wasn't ever the way she was. And that you can't live in the past even if you want to.* From my desk in Bellingham I nod and then from her desk in Columbia Larissa nods and then we sign off. Although being that I'm in the midst of a burgeoning one, I talked with her about relationships today, more often when I talk with Larissa now we discuss professional concerns or social ones. How adjuncting can be so relentlessly soul-crushing, or that it's so much more expensive here as compared to in Missouri. How I'm still not sure why I feel the need to be constantly productive when the end result so often leaves me wanting still more. Demisexuality, attachment theory, and why I think pondering both might be important. And then I listen to her talk about why reading is overrated—I should take up running or aikido or hip-hop dance or enroll in another improv class—and how she can't seem to find a good pair of wireless earbuds. She's my therapist, Larissa, and the counsel that she gives me is always worthwhile. But it's when she starts talking about her own problems or forgets what she previously said to me (my memory of her saying *What you're doing is trying to hide that you might be wrong* differs from hers, in that she claims that she never said such a thing, would never say something like it to a patient of hers) before saying a variant on that same thing again—this is when I gain the most knowledge from Larissa. It's an inconsistency that would, I know, drive other people mad and on glass half-empty days it does so for me also. But more often this errancy of Larissa's reminds me that the process of change can be a lifelong one, and that perhaps what makes her the best therapist for me isn't what I say but how Larissa hears it and, in hearing, responds. Unsparingly, warmly, stout cold care.

Same as ever, Larissa quotes Yogi Berra before we part virtual ways. *Don't worry about making too many wrong mistakes.* As usual I nod, say I'll try. I'm beginning to understand that what's considered wrong by some people isn't a mistake, not at all. I'm learning.

*

Never out loud but always omnipresent in bold black letters, what Larissa says between the lines during every session of ours is something I already know and still, on most days, actively try to forget—that I am not terminally unique, that whatever they might be my problems are commonplace. That across the board I'm very lucky to have the minor, silly problems that I do.

Perhaps perversely, knowing this gives me hope.

*

XIV. The easy attainment of love makes it of little value; difficulty of attainment makes it prized.

*

"Every man is not only himself. Men are lived over again. There was none then but there hath been someone since that parallels him, and is as it were his revived self" imparts Sir Thomas Browne in *Religio Medici.*

*

The revived self, afresh. An entirely new person. Who knows where it will go?

*

"I've got my hands on the one end/ And I don't know where to put them" The Promise Ring sings on "How Nothing Feels."

The only difference between the first time I heard that song, though, and when I listen now is that this unknowing is a comfort, a source of strength. Nothing feels until you let it.

*

For Millennials, sexual prolificity matters less than personal identity, comfort and security does. I'm selfish for my self, in other words, but only in relation to who I imagine my best self can be.

This Millennial sexual predilection is a big deal—or not. "…everything pertaining to sex has been a 'special case' in our culture, evoking peculiarly inconsistent attitudes" wrote Susan Sontag in her essay "The Pornographic Imagination," included in her 1969 collection *Styles of Radical Will.* In that instance Sontag was referencing sexual behavior as a means of virtue—then and now, the less people you do it with the more virtuous you are, at least to most swathes of society—but more important to me is the thoroughness of the inconsistency. Sexuality-based generational norms and standards matter far less, in the end, than stable and solidified ways of being. Millennials are lazy and entitled; Millennials are driven and determined. Vapidly greedy, Millennials are selfish; hyperaware of the struggles they are facing and will face, Millennials are selfless. And the list goes on. All of these things and none of them, Millennials like myself are and will continue to be. There's no one way, no single generalization that solves a problem that didn't exist in the first place. Selfhood is as malleable as one's sexuality, one's sexual nature. We are constantly losing our self to our selves. Therein lies the elliptical power of its beauty.

*

"I feel promiscuous but maybe I'm a prude" Daddy Issues sings on "I'm Not." For years I lived that life and then one morning I stopped showing up for it. In finely sliced filaments, the future's still arriving.

*

Does that make sense?

*

"Perhaps/ The truth depends on a walk around a lake" states Wallace Stevens in "Notes Toward a Supreme Fiction." Walking, always walking, I can see the lake and its surroundings in all their splendorous veracity.

*

Seven years before publishing "The Pornographic Imagination" Sontag wrote "The mind is a whore" in her journal. What a way to believe, to imagine! She made her daimon work for her and the world took notes.

*

Instead of leaving the box, I shall enclose my own ever-changing world within it, making a vast life out of what was previously just four enclosed corners, top to bottom, floor to ceiling, back to front.

*

Nothing's shocking except the ability to change oneself. When I listen to Jane's Addiction's album *Nothing's Shocking* now that's what I hear.

*

I haven't read a book in a month! My eyes just as often lift up now, not down.

*

Last night I kissed the woman I'm currently seeing goodnight and she smiled at me. Although I did, I didn't know what to do or say or think. So I kissed her again.

*

And yet.

May 2018- November 2018

April 2021-May 2021

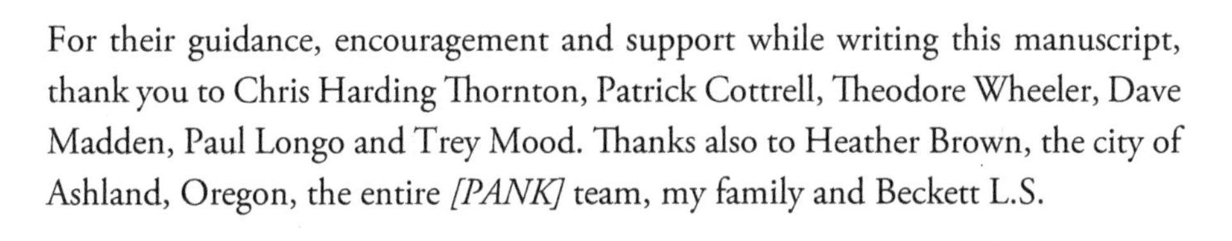
For their guidance, encouragement and support while writing this manuscript, thank you to Chris Harding Thornton, Patrick Cottrell, Theodore Wheeler, Dave Madden, Paul Longo and Trey Mood. Thanks also to Heather Brown, the city of Ashland, Oregon, the entire *[PANK]* team, my family and Beckett L.S.

Thank you.

Excerpts from this book were originally published in *Fence* and the *Cleveland Review of Books*. Thank you to Claire Donato, Nik Slackman and Zach Peckham.

To hear a section of *And Yet* recited by the author, please text the # 775 240 7347 with the message And Yet. From there, await further communiques.

About the Author

Jeff Alessandrelli is most recently the author of the poetry collection *Fur Not Light* (2019), which *The Kenyon Review* called an "example of radical humility… its poems enact a quiet but persistent empathy in the world of creative writing." *Entitled Nothing of the Month Club*, an expanded version of *Fur Not Light* was released in the United Kingdom in 2021. In addition to his writing Alessandrelli also directs the nonprofit book press/record label Fonograf Editions. jeffalessandrelli.net

CPSIA information can be obtained
at www.ICGtesting.com
Printed in the USA
BVHW092127100922
646699BV00002B/121